THE IMPEACHED PRESIDENT

The Reluctant President Vol. 5

JACK R. STANLEY

Wrightbridge Press

TWO FREE E-BOOKS

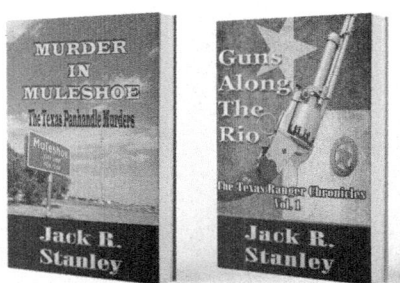

[Murder in Muleshoe]
If you were murdered would they try to find the killer or plan him a parade?

[Guns Along The Rio]
In 1858, two fresh-off-the-ranch 17-year-olds join the Texas Rangers. What could possibly go wrong?

GO TO: http://eepurl.com/dKEi_Y

The Impeached President
(The Reluctant President Vol 5)

Copyright © 2022 by Jack R. Stanley.
All rights reserved
ISBN: 978-1-954212-52-7

This book may not be copied or reproduced, in whole or in part, by any means, electronic, mechanical, or otherwise, without written permission from the publisher except by a reviewer who may quote brief passages in his/her review.

This is a work of fiction. Any resemblance to any persons, events, or localities is purely coincidental and beyond the intent of the author and publisher.

Credits:
Edited by
Mary Lee Stanley
and
Rose Marie Reed

Wrightbridge Press

jacks@wrightbridgepress.com
www.thefictionwritersnotebook.com
www.jackrstanley.com

To the love of my life
Mary Lee
who makes all things possible.

CHAPTER 1

The Secretary of Health and Human Services, along with three PhDs, stood in front of President Porter Randall's Oval Office desk. The words that grabbed the President's attention were, "..pandemic — worse than the Flu of 1918."

As a former multi-tour Army doctor in Afghanistan, 52-year-old, second term Independent, Porter Randle, was no stranger to the ideas of population ravaging epidemics and pandemics. He had been a surgeon, but prior to his first deployment to the middle-east, he emersed himself in a brief study of the microorganisms behind these maladies. He was fortifying himself against their potential in the third world, where he was headed.

With his mind for history, numbers and dates, Porter tried to recall part of what he knew about such ravages while also listening to the professionals in front of him at the same time.

The pathogens of plagues are older than humanity. Bacteria evolved 3.5 billion years ago versus 1.5 billion for viruses. Humans didn't appear until 130,000 years ago. God's curses on ancient Egypt were more than diseases. But the plagues of humankind had been of 3 significant types — bubonic, pneumonic, and septicemic.

The bubonic revealed itself with furuncles, puss-filled skin abscesses on the neck, and the armpits and groin that would grow and turn black. Thus the name Black Death. The disease that first appeared in China 2,600 years ago still exists in Madagascar and reemerges there every year.

The pneumonic plagues attacked the lungs of its victims, while the septicemic affected the blood of its targets. It was 100% fatal if not caught and treated. There had been less than 100 cases in the US in the last 50 years. Some professionals referred to these as "the Disney Plagues." They were all carried by rats, prairie dogs, rabbits, squirrels, and chipmunks — all favorite characters for the animation studio.

The oldest of the type, the bubonic, was a bacterium that attacked the lymph nodes. Once there, it produced the swollen and soon blackened buboes. Without treatment, the disease could spread to other parts of the body until it caused death.

The difference between a pandemic and an epidemic was the spread of the disease. Epidemics were localized, while pandemics knew no regions or borders. There had been six plagues in history.

The plague of Justinian reached Constantinople in 542 BC. The outbreak swept throughout the Mediterranean world for another 225 years, finally disappearing in 750 BC. Justinian, the first, reigned over the Byzantine Empire. He was one of the most important late Roman and Byzantine emperors. Millions died from the plague. Medical historians say it originated in China. Yet it traveled across northeast India and was even carried to the Great Lakes of Africa via overland and sea trade routes. The Byzantine historian Procopius of Caesarea claimed the point of origin for Justinian's plague was Egypt on the Nile River's northern and eastern shores. Later research claimed the disease spread north to Alexandria and east to Palestine. In total, twenty-four million lives were lost to the disease.

Then came the bubonic plague, also known as Black Death. Twelve ships arrived from the Black Sea and docked in a Sicilian port in 1347. The majority of the sailors aboard each vessel were dead. Those still alive were covered in black boils that oozed blood and pus. Authorities ordered the fleet of "death ships" back out to sea. However, it was too late. The bubonic plague spread across Europe and Asia for the next five years. In the mid-1300s, over 20 million people in Europe alone — almost a third of the population would perish.

Upwards of 80–95 percent of the Native American population was decimated within the first 150 years following 1492. Unknowingly, European explorers brought smallpox, measles, and other viruses to the New World, whose inhabitants had no immunity. Smallpox was the biggest killer of them all.

The Great Plague of London was an epidemic that ravaged the city for a year, 1665 to 1666. Officially, over 68,500 people died during the epidemic, though historians place the actual deaths in excess of 100,000 at a time. This was when the city's population was estimated at 460,000. The disappearance of the plague was attributed to the Great Fire of London in September 1666. That event almost cast the plague into the forgotten bin of history. However, scholars today generally agree that the end of the plague was spontaneous.

The bubonic plague struck for a third time in the Yunnan province in China around 1855. Then, it recurred in successive waves as it spread to Canton, Macao, and Hong Kong in 1894. This became the world's first true pandemic as it applied to all the inhabited continents. It claimed over 20 million lives and was not considered over until 1960, when less than 200 people died annually from the disease.

The cholera pandemic from 1846 to 1860 was the third major outbreak of that disease. It originated in India. When it reached Russia, the epidemic became a pandemic and claimed over one million lives. In London, cholera took over 10,000 lives. Of all the 19th-century epidemics, this pandemic was considered to have had the highest fatalities in Asia, Europe, Africa, and North America. Finally, it was British physician John Snow, laboring in a poor area of London, who identified contaminated water as the means of transmitting the disease.

Finally, the 1918 influenza pandemic was ranked as the most severe pandemic in recent history. Caused by an H1N1 virus, it had genes of avian origin. It spread worldwide from 1918 to 1919. There is still no consensus about the source of the disease to this day. It was first identified in returning World War I military personnel in the US. About 500 million people, or one-third of the world's population, became infected with this disease. The number of deaths was estimated to be at least 50 million worldwide. Notably, people younger than 5 years, 20-40 years old, and 65 and older exhibited the highest mortality. A unique feature of this pandemic was the high mortality in healthy people, including those in the 20-40 year age group.

As he was recalling these grim statistics in his mind, the President ushered his guests to the couches in the middle of the Oval Office to continue their discussion.

CHAPTER 2

Porter found it a little odd that the 63-year-old Dr. Sinead Trench, PhD and MD, Director of the National Institute of Allergies and Infectious Diseases, spoke on behalf of the trio of health professionals. This also included the Secretary of Health and Human Services (HHS). Dr. Trench was willowy, exquisitely, yet tastefully dressed, in a muted professional suit accented with a jeweled broach. Contrary to her appearance, the woman was aggressive and assertive. She seemed to be driven to explain the situation at hand.

The second physician in the group was Dr. Judson Whitehead, Director of the National Institute of Health, and Dr. Trench's boss. Whitehead reminded the President of the Muppet character Beaker. The NIH director wore a suit accented by a bow tie. He had flyaway red hair on top of his almost 7-foot frame. He was only slightly less emaciated than that of a concentration camp victim.

The trio's third member of the MDs was a diminutive black lady of sixty-five, Laurennie Jarry. She had white hair cut close to her head, a soft round face, and wire-framed bifocals. Something about Dr. Jarry projected an air of confidence and knowledge. Porter suspected that although she didn't speak often, people listened when she did. Her title was Director of the National Institute of Biomedical Imaging and Bioengineering.

All the physicians were part of the Centers for Disease Control and Prevention — the CDC — an agency under HHS.

Talmage Goughenbaugh, Porter's Secretary of HHS, was 58, squat with a goatee and blue eyes. Porter understood that Goughenbaugh ran his agency, letting each department function with a great deal of autonomy, yet with no hesitation of stepping in when required. He was known as a problem-solving pragmatist. He, too, listened more than he spoke — which made his few words worth hearing.

Also attending was Porter's Chief-of-Staff, Graham Newcome — Porter's White House Chief-of-Staff. The always suitably dressed 32-year-old Newcome had been with Porter when he served in Congress as a Representative from the Texas Panhandle. The rail-thin, pock-marked face, Presidential assistant had light blue eyes and a quick mind.

The five officials sat on the couches, Goughenbaugh at the opposite end of the divan Graham had taken. Drs. Trench, Jarry, and Whitehead sat across from them. Trench took the position nearest the couch across from Sec. Goughenbaugh. Porter sat in one of a pair of easy chairs at either end of couch grouping.

"What do we know at this point?" Porter asked.

"That it's a rapidly spreading coronavirus," Dr. Trench said. "The public health people in Wuhan, China, sent out the warning only hours ago."

"We've designated it as SARS-CoV-2," Dr. Whitehead said with his Adam's apple bobbing. "It appears to be a pneumonia type of disease."

"As I understand it, we have no known drugs to fight it. No protocols for treatment," Secretary Goughenbaugh spoke for the second time, "and no idea which populations are most vulnerable."

Dr. Trench asserted herself again and pointed out, "We do not have any confirmed cases in the continental U.S., Alaska, or any of our territories. We only know it exists.

"One thing we do know," Dr. Jarry said quietly, "is that it's going to be a pandemic."

Trench took control again, adding, "Like, or worse than, the Spanish Flu of 1918."

Sec. Goughenbaugh said, "There simply appears to be more we don't know than the few facts we do."

"We know," Dr. Trench said, "that the typical annual flu is avian in origin. Avian influenza — Type A. It occurs naturally among wild aquatic birds worldwide. The virus is easily transferred to ducks, geese, and swans. It jumps to humans when people handle these types of birds — feeding, and selling these birds in open markets — stepping in bird poop or touching infected birds — people with cuts or open lacerations of every type — and the virus develops into a human transmittable disease. Person to person — people get on trains, boats, planes — and it becomes an epidemic and then a pandemic."

"What are your recommendations at this moment?" Porter asked.

No one wanted to step into this question, so it was up to Sec. Goughenbaugh to admit, "We don't have any yet. This is an emergency advisory notice only, Mr. President."

"Then the one thing we don't want to do is start a nationwide panic," Porter said.

"Agreed," Drs. Trench, Jarry, and Whitehead said in unison.

Dr. Sinead Trench said, "We are gearing up our staffs and need to do everything we can to prepare for this — even though we're not sure what all those steps are. We are working closely with the World Health Organization."

"If this hits like the Spanish Flu," Whitehead added, sitting forward, "we are looking at not only hospital overcrowding -- but possibly even bodies stacked up beyond what mortuary can handle. So we should be ready with protective gear from doctors, nurses, EMTs, and others who will be directly in contact with the patients."

"Let me get my communications people on this," Porter said. "It seems we will need to roll out an announcement at some point. I'd like to be ready on an instant's notice. After that, we should be ready to send the word out in whatever form turns out to be the best."

"Thank you, Mr. President," Secretary Goughenbaugh said, checking to see if there were any other suggestions from his two physicians. "I don't know what else we can ask."

"Well, I'm thinking we need to get the military in the loop on this," Porter said. "And perhaps some of our manufacturing execs to up the production of — what — gowns, gloves, surgical masks?"

"M-95 masks in particular," Dr. Jarry said. "They'll be the most effective."

"Of course," Porter nodded. "How about HAZMAT gear?"

"That, too," she said, checking with her colleague, Dr. Whitehead, who nodded his agreement. "But we don't know if it will be that variant or not yet."

"Then," Porter suggested, "how about setting up a task force of people who can help — from a broad range of fields? We can add to this as we need."

"Excellent idea," Mr. President," his Secretary of Health and Human Services acknowledged.

"You keep your feelers out and your sources alert," the President said with finality. "Let's reconvene in — when the situation changes."

The doctors agreed and stood with the Secretary. The meeting was over.

Porter took a few moments alone with Graham Newcome in the Oval Office, discussing what they had just learned. Then, when they were sure they both understood the situation, Porter pressed the button on his intercom to his personal secretary, Gwendolyn Jacobs.

"Miss Jacobs, could you please contact Vice President Holyoak and ask her to join me as soon as possible?"

"Yes, Sir."

"Also, ask Miss Fontana and Mr. Sterling to join us when the Vice President arrives."

"Right away, Sir."

"How's the love life going?" Porter asked Graham as they waited. Porter's Chief-of-Staff was in love with Cinnamon Higdon, Porter's former Director of White House Communications. She was now an Associate Professor of journalism at the University of Missouri - Columbia, the nation's first journalism school. The pair were spending hours in the air, flying back and forth between DC and Columbia, Missouri, to spend time together.

"About as well as could be expected," Graham said. "She's always up to her chin in papers to grade and academic duties she never imagined. But at least twice a month, we manage to find some time."

"Good for you both," Porter smiled.

Vice President Tracy Holyoak had been a three-term libertarian representative from Wyoming. She had been Porter and his wife Deidra's choice for VP when Porter decided to seek the Presidency in the most recent election. The 38-year-old, 4 foot 11-inch ash-blonde entered the President's office 15 minutes later.

"You rang?" she joked, trying to close the door, her dark hazel eyes flashing with wit.

But Howard X. Sterling grabbed and held the door for Saundra Fontana. Howard, White House Press Secretary, was a former Intercontinental News Key on-the-air anchor and three-time Pulitzer Prize-winning broadcast journalist. He was wearing a starched buttoned-down light blue shirt with a dark tie and vest.

Saundra Fontana, Head of White House Communications, was a middle-aged blonde with hints of gray at her roots. She had been Howard's longtime producer and head writer. She was a pleasant-looking woman who was serious and intelligent.

"I think the gang's all here," Porter said as he ushered all four to the couches. "You all are aware of the Spanish Flu infection of 1918? I've just been informed that we're about to face something similar — possibly even worse.

"First off, Vice President Holyoak, I'm appointing you to lead a Task Force on what, so far, we're calling COVID. That name may change — but it stands for 'coronavirus disease.' The CDC is telling me they've been notified of a new strand in China. It is rapidly spreading and very contagious. It very well could turn out to be a pandemic like we've not seen since the Spanish Flu. We don't know more about it than what I've just told you. For the moment, I'd like you to compile a list of people you think should be on this — where, when, and how often to meet."

"There is space in the Executive Office building," Tracy Holyoak said.

"Secretary Goughenbaugh should be one person you'll want. Expand or eliminate as you see fit. But consider the needs of those who will be front-line workers — in hospitals, clinics, even hospice workers — EMTs — first responders who will need information — perhaps a website — 1- 800 number. Then supplies. What will be needed, and who can we rely on to provide personal protective equipment — it's known as PPE in medical circles — and whatever medical devices might be required? I'm thinking ventilators for the worst case victims. And consider how every step we take will cascade and what's likely to come next. Make use of the military for anything you might need."

"And let's not forget the resources of the VA medical centers," Graham spoke up.

"Thank you, Graham," the President said. "That's a power we rarely tap." Then, the President turned back to his communication team.

"There are no cases we know of in the US yet. So rather than putting out some announcement of things-to-come, I'd like us to be ready with a public notice — with facts and informed recommendations at any moment. This could leak out anytime — and I don't want to be accused of hiding anything."

"Who are our contacts?" the Vice President asked.

The President handed each of the three a slip of paper with the names of Secretary Goughenbaugh and Doctors Sinead Trench. Laurennie Jarry and Judson Whitehead, along with each person's title.

"Beyond what I've just told you," Porter said, "this is going to be a day-by-day, even hour-by-hour challenge. We'll all be learning as we go."

CHAPTER 3

The President's impeachment trial in the Senate ended with a whimper. Porter had been accused of corruption and contributing to ethnic cleansing in Croatia. However, after the testimony of Dr. Nikola Novak, the surgeon and hospital administer in Zagreb, Croatia, and a vote by the jury, the US Senate, all charges were dismissed. The fact was Porter had given money to Croatia — but it had been to establish a state-of-the-art surgery suite in the premier hospital in Zagreb. His contribution had nothing to do with ethnic cleansing.

House Speaker Vincent Sturges was humiliated after his accusations of Porter's motive in Croatia in the early 90s fell flat.

This was the third time the Speaker felt President Randall had wronged him. First was when acting as interim Speaker of the House, Porter was suddenly thrust into the White House with the unexpected death of then-President Leo V. Gibson. There had been no replacement vice president nominated to fill the void left by the scandalized previous holder who had resigned, and thus, there was none in office. Sturges became the new Speaker of the House within a week and still felt he should have ascended to the presidency. Next was Porter's refusing to accept the Republican nomination for the presidency at the next election cycle. The party's choice then fell to Sturges. Finally, when Porter entered the national contest as an independent candidate, all the pundits and professional political gurus believed he had no choice. But Sturges and the Democratic nominee were soundly beaten in the election and mortified by Porter's margin of victory.

The Speaker left the Senate chamber but stopped to answer a single media question about the decision.

"The process has been completed. But regardless of the outcome, history will always cite Porter Randall as an impeached president. That scarlet letter has been hung around his neck, and he can neither deny it nor ignore it."

With that, Sturges started to walk away calmly, but stopped and turned back as he said, "This is not over." However, his animosity toward the President continued to fester deep inside.

The collapse of the impeachment attempt by Porter's political enemies was the lead story early in the day. Most of the media labored to downplay the stupidity of the lame attempt to remove President Randall. However, by prime time, another story had taken over the number one position.

Duri Yoo told his wife Bae not to confront the large black man, who often stumbled into their convenience store on Holgate Boulevard in Portland, Oregon. The first generation North Korean defector and once North Korean soldier, Duri had worked tirelessly to create a new life for himself in America. He had been wounded twice in his brazen daylight escape across the DMZ. He recovered in a South Korean hospital for three months and was granted permission to emigrate to the US.

His wife, Bae, third-generation Korean-American, was attracted to Duri's work ethic and sense of humor as he struggled to learn the language and the American way of life. With the help of Bae's family, she and Duri were able to purchase a convenience store from a retiring owner. They had upgraded the store into a modern and popular business in the mixed ethnic neighborhood. The couple was known for giving credit to elders on a fixed income — and even forgiving debts at times.

Michael Robertson had always been big. In grade school, he was the butt of many a joke. But in middle school, his size proved to be an asset on the football team. His high school days were his golden years. The 300-pound defensive guard had even picked up a loose football and scored the winning touchdown in the state finals. Michael made the Oregon all-state high school team and was awarded a full-ride football scholarship to OU, the University of Oregon, and Eugene's public flagship research university. However, Michael was no scholar. He was used to being passed from class to class, grade to grade, because of his importance to the football squad. He only lasted one and a half semesters at college before he flunked out, failing all his classes except football.

With no job skills, no ambitions, and addicted to the popularity of high school, the young man found even street gang life to be more than he could endure. So he became a drug and alcohol abuser and began bullying his way through life.

The day President Randall was exonerated of his impeachment charges, a shirtless Michael Robertson wandered into the Yoo's Street Mart. To satisfy his munchies, Michael grabbed a generic 6-liter bottle of soda from the shelf and a hand full of candy bars.

Bae yelled at him as he barged past the counter and opened the door to the street. He shot her the finger with his middle digit of the hand holding the plastic bottle.

Robertson staggered across 92nd Avenue and slammed a dint into the hood of Matías Desoto's Toyota Corolla, blocking traffic. The shirtless man banged on other cars as he ripped open candy bars and stuffed them into his mouth. He seemed disoriented. Two drivers and three pedestrians called 911.

By the time police arrived, a single officer in a squad car, Michael Robertson had entered a nearby city park. Officer Bent Song, fifth-generation Chinese/American, parked his car at the curb and left his flashing lights on as he followed the huge black man into the park.

Three gunshots were heard, and when a crowd gathered, Michael Robertson was dead on the sidewalk, what was left of his soda spilling onto the concrete.

Liberal local and national news headlines proclaimed this to be another instance of a white cop killing an innocent black man.

CHAPTER 4

By nightfall in Portland, the narrative was active that the "gentle giant" Michael Robertson, had been gunned down by a white cop out of the site of everyone for no reason. Robertson was portrayed as a local hero, football star and beloved member of the black community. Black smoke funneled to the sky from piles of old tires burning in the middle of downtown Portland. The crowd of mourners at the city park had grown into a belligerent mob carrying Black Lives Matter signs, lead by ANTIFA members, in full black riot gear. Car windows were smashed, Molotov cocktails thrown at business fronts, and looting had begun.

Totally unprepared for the situation, the Portland police were back on its heels as three squad cars were torched. Patrol officers, black, Hispanic, Asian, and white, were dragged from their vehicles and escaped with their lives only by fleeing.

The carnage continued through the night as police and media helicopters circled the expanding rabble as it roamed and destroyed unchecked. The developing narrative said that innocent Michael Robertson dropped to his knees and surrendered to the officer, who then fired three shots into the submissive victim. "I'm no threat — don't shoot" became the slogan for the protest. The words first appeared scrawled by hand on handheld cardboard signs. Within hours, the same motto was on professionally printed, perfectly spaced, type set white placards and street wide cloth banners.

At a morning protest using the raised platform for a bronze statue of a deer, organizers with bull horns gave voice to the slogan, which was parroted back by the crowd.

"I'm no threat — don't shoot!"

The mayor attended tried to appease the crowd by claiming he was on their side and wanted to get to the truth of the killing. But he was shouted down and embarrassed when he was pelted with bottles of urine and shot with yellow paint balls. The Portland police chief refused to release the body camera footage of the officer who shot Robertson. The officer's name was withheld, and the police claimed to be trying to protect evidence for a fair public hearing.

Social media blew up with the hashtag, "I'm no threat — don't shoot." Main stream media proclaimed this event to be a murder-by-cop against someone whose only crime was living-while-black.

At the White House Daily Press Briefing, Howard Sterling responded to the media's questions as if he were still America's Most Trusted News Anchor.

"The President has not been in touch with the mayor of Portland nor authorities in Oregon. This is not, I repeat, *not* a federal matter. The President has no interest in extending the power of the national government into affairs that rightfully belong in the hands of local and state officials. If, however, any other level of government wishes federal help, the President stands ready to help in any way legally available.

"The President is aware of the situation in Portland — but has no intention of overstepping his authority to intervene. As it says in the 10th Amendment of the Constitution — 'The powers not delegated to the United States by the Constitution, nor prohibited by it to the States, are reserved to the states respectively, or to the people.'

"The Portland Police, The Oregon State Police, and the National Guard are available should they be needed. But their need and use is the providence of Portland and Oregon authorities — not the federal government."

Howard looked up from his notes before he said, "The President has no comment on the events because he does not want to put his thumb on the scales of justice. There appears to be ample evidence in the incident and even body cam footage of the actual shooting — none of which have been released. The President's only hope is for justice — whatever that turns out to be."

The first question came from a reporter from one of the left-leaning cable networks. "Has the President telephoned the mother of Michael Robertson to express grief to his mother for losing her son — as he would for a fallen American service member?"

"Are you," Howard answered, "under the impression that Michael Roberts was somehow working in the service of his country?"

"Well ... no," the dumpy reporter stammered, trying to recover, "... but he is an American — a black American — who the police have murdered."

"Was he murdered? What is your evidence? No such information has reached the White House. Is it your network's verdict that this incident was murder? Have you tried the police officer in question and found him guilty? Where did you get the authority to try and judge him? And whatever became of the concept of innocent until proven guilty?"

"He was white — and the victim was black."

"Is that all the evidence you need? No more context? No more facts? Just, he's black, and the shooter was white? And, for your information — something all of you in the journalism profession should already know -- the officer was not Caucasian — he was Asian-American. Actually, he was just an American. So was the young man who was killed.

"But you have judged an officer in the performance of his duty as wrong and guilty of a crime? Why? Because of his skin color? If you get assaulted on your way home tonight, are you going to call the police for help? Or you going to assume the officer is guilty of some offense, even if they get there in time to arrest your attacker?"

"But it is a racial crime!" a woman from a big city newspaper called out.

"When there's a DUI car wreck, if one driver is black and the other is white, is that automatically a racial crime? Would it make any difference which driver was in the wrong?

"Don't you people understand what journalism is supposed to be about? Truth-telling. 'All we want are the facts, ma'am,' as Sgt. Joe Friday used to say on Dragnet. What are the facts? All the facts — not only the ones that fit your narrative. Are you ready to publish your opinions as facts? Is your story complete without seeing the evidence? The President isn't. He's holding an open mind — questioning — but open?"

Of course, this was not sufficient for the reporters in the briefing, and several tried different tactics to elicit a response, but Howard gave none. He even ignored some questions and reporters moving on to others who understood and accepted the White House's position — for the moment.

That night riots occurred again in Portland, with sympathetic riots in Seattle, San Francisco, Chicago, Detroit, Cleveland, and Atlanta. The Portland mayor attempted to speak to a gathering crowd in a city park, expressing his sympathy and even support for the public upset. But he was first shouted down, then peppered with rotten fruit and vegetables before being hit by plastic bottles of urine. Finally, the mayor retreated and was shielded by his police bodyguards.

By the third night, the unrest had spread to Dallas, Kansas City, and other cities. The crowds resorted to throwing Molotov Cocktails, breaking windows and storefronts in each case. At first, big box stores were looted, and smaller businesses were set ablaze.

Finally, the Portland police released the body camera footage of the

Michael Robertson confrontation. In it, the voice of the unnamed officer is heard shouting at Robertson. The big black man staggered down the park sidewalk, not responding. Then, as the officer appeared to get closer, Robertson stopped and turned, bleary-eyed, toward the officer.

"Police! Halt! Raise your hands!" the officer commanded.

Michael Robertson didn't appear to understand. He took a big gulp of the cola bottle in his paw.

"Did you hear me?" the officer asked. "Police! Raise your hands!"

"Fuck you, cop!" Robertson blurted, and turned away.

"You are under arrest! Stop! Get down on your knees and put your hands behind your head!"

The huge black man stumbled on, paying no attention.

The officer's service revolver, a Glock 19, was seen in his hands, pointed down at the sidewalk. One hand released the weapon as he reached for the microphone velcroed to his uniform's shoulder.

"Officer 614. Code 78. East sidewalk McMurry Park," the officer's voice was heard saying.

The code and location were heard as it was repeated over the officer's radio by the dispatcher. Three responses were called in and heard on the officer's receiver.

With both hands again on his semi-automatic, the officer followed the staggering Robertson again, ordering him to stop and get down on his knees. The big man stumbled on a few more steps and then stopped. He half-turned and squinted at the officer. Then Robertson flung his half-empty bottle of soda at the officer — hitting the police officer in the chest and spewing brown liquid on the lens of the body camera.

But even as the lens cleared, it was clear Michael Robertson was taking a stance to confront the officer. Sirens of other approaching police cars were heard. The officer stopped and repeated his orders.

"You are under arrest! Get on your knees and put your hands behind your head!"

The hulking former football player did what had always worked for him. Michael Robertson bull-rushed the officer, who tried to step aside. But he was grabbed by a big hand and slung to the ground.

"Stop!!" the officer yelled as the monster came to stand over him, snarling and spitting.

In his mind, this was the big game — for the title. Michael had the quarterback down, but the QB still had the ball. Michael's job was to crush the man with his size and weight.

As Michael Robertson lunged, the officer fired once, which paused the big man, but he renewed his efforts and pounced. The officer fired twice more before the lens of the body camera was obscured by the attacker's body.

The footage ended there.

The media quickly found the officer's number and then published his name, ignored his race, but posted his address, phone number, and email.

CHAPTER 5

Vice President Tracy Holyoak assembled a list of people for the COVID Task Force. She worked with her Chief-of-Staff, Darla Ritter. Ritter, Tracy's former campaign manager, was blonde and anything but fragile. She was an intelligent orb of energy with a quick smile that was friendly but not flirty. She was focused and spoke in bell clear voice which carried authority without being demanding or offensive.

"Are we ready to start meeting?" Darla asked. "Do I need to find a space and set a schedule?" Her head was down, checking the potential Task Force members' list on her Android tablet.

"Not yet," the Vice President answered. "But do contact everyone we've listed and let's be sure they're willing and able to serve."

"Will do," the Chief-of-Staff said, almost jumping to her feet and heading for the door.

"Oh," Tracy called, "Ask Harm to give me an undisturbed half hour." Harm Bell was her executive secretary who manned the desk outside the VP's office. The former linebacker on one of her husband, Bradley's high school state championship teams, could have been a biker bar bouncer instead of a fully licensed member of the Wyoming bar association. Now, he was a secretary to the Vice President and learning the ropes of national politics.

"Got it," Darla answered as she stepped out and closed the door behind her.

The moment she was alone, Tracy reached into her purse and fished out the silver yet-to-be publicly released Pi phone. First, she glanced at her watch, which read 11 AM. Then she activated the satellite phone and punched in the first of three pre-programmed numbers into the device. After two rings, a man's voice answered.

"Yeah, what?" the voice said.

"Is this Ivan?" Tracy asked.

"Ain't no Ivan here, man," the man said and hung up.

Tracy clicked off and put the phone back deep in her purse.

This entire conversation was in code. She had called David Royal, known to the few who knew him as The Vice President's Man. The secretive former Delta Force and Secret Service member was a man who went by many names and had several ready-made entire identities in the event he needed one.

The call was to another Pi phone of only a half dozen currently in use. The Vice President had called the unlisted number and said the name, Ivan. All that mattered was the first two letters of this name — I and V — Roman numerals, IV. It meant "Can you meet me at four o'clock?" The man's response, "Ain't no Ivan here," confirmed "the secret space behind a wall in the Vice President's study at four was a set."

The Vice President had office space in the West Wing building where the President's Oval Office was, but Tracy Holyoak preferred the more spacious Ceremonial Vice President's office in the Eisenhower Executive Office Building (EEOB).

The five-floor granite structure with slate, copper, and cast iron trim, had four wings and two rectangular courtyards. The open spaces were separated by a transversing central branch that linked the east and west wings.

Its been referred to as the architect's infant asylum and by President Harry S. Truman as "the greatest monstrosity in America." One architectural historian, however, described it as "perhaps the best extant example in America of the second empire." The building survived calls for its demolition in the 1920s and again in 1980. Built between 1871 and 1888, the EEOB was initially designated the Departments of State, War, and Navy.

The General Services Administration maintained the 553 room building. It was currently occupied by members of the President's staff and that of the Vice President.

In 1981, suites of all the "secretary of" were restored. This included the VP's office and study.

Three known basement levels were acknowledged, but it had been speculated there were others. The Vice President's man, Richard Royal, entered the elaborate D.C. underground tunnel complex with a military name tag reading Givens. He was dressed in an Army Lt. Colonel's uniform with a briefcase in one hand. Such officers were prolific, walking and riding golf carts to and fro in the system.

The 34-year-old, 6 feet 2 inches tall solid 185-pound man, was waiting when the Vice President opened a bookcase in her study to the hidden but lighted passage.

"Madam Vice President," he said when Tracy crossed into the space.

"Colonel — Givens," she said, reading his name tag. "I would like for you to continue your investigation into Irving Zaddach. I've been studying the pictures and your notes. It's clear to me that some terrible things are happening to some innocent young women — if not children."

Zaddach was a popular figure in elite circles and even in political, financial, and entertainment fields. However, the source of his income was vague.

"The link to Jerren Glowicki is worrying," she added.

Glowicki, a mysterious Polish-born figure of enormous wealth, had an anti-American bent and supported organizations and people who shared his views. However, he stayed secluded due to a rare genetic skin condition that caused red, scaly skin.

"What we need is evidence which would hold up in court. Zaddach has already skated on one pedophilia charge. So if anything can be done against him, it will have to hold up to heavy public scrutiny.

The gray-eyed, dark auburn-haired colonel nodded his understanding. "It could take some time to piece this puzzle together."

"Please, do what you can."

"Yes, ma'am."

Their meeting was over. The officer saluted, and the Vice President returned the gesture. Then she turned and stepped back into her office. On a middle shelf, she tipped a beautifully leather-bound and gold titled copy of Pilgrim's Progress back upright. The bookcase rotated and swung back into place.

CHAPTER 6

The first case of the new COVID infection was reported in Washington State. A US-based company sales associate returned from a trip to Wuhan, China. The 35-year-old man checked into a Seattle urgent care clinic after seeing reports about the outbreak in the news. He experienced a cough, fever, nausea, and vomiting and was hospitalized. His condition grew worse, and he developed pneumonia.

In their next meeting with the President, Doctors Trench, Jarry, and Whitehead, plus Sec. Goughenbaugh reported on the first known American case. Vice President Tracy Holyoak was in attendance, seated beside the President's Chief Of Staff, Graham Newcome, in the chairs opposite the President at the end of the double couches. The medical team's account of events ended with the fact that the Seattle men's symptoms abated after ten days in the hospital.

Again, Dr. Sinead Trench, the refined and smartly dressed Director of the National Institute of Allergies and Infectious Diseases, took the lead with a striking broach on her jacket. "This is only the first of what we can expect to be millions of similar cases."

"But it is survivable," Porter said.

"At least in this one case," Dr. Trench agreed. "Perhaps it is by those in his age bracket, current health — ethnicity — we simply don't know what the parameters are to be survivable."

"We are watching to see if the Seattle area will become the epicenter of the infection," Dr. Whitehead said, still looking like a living Muppet character.

"You have seen my proposed list of people to be on the Task Force," Vice President Holyoak said, handing out a single printout page to the visitors as well as to the President. "I've included those whom all of you have suggested. Unless you have other suggestions, I want to convene a meeting of this panel on Monday."

The HHS Secretary and the physicians all agreed.

"Any policy suggestions?" Porter asked.

Dr. Trench answered for the group, "Not yet, Mr. President."

"Are we ready to announce what we expect?" he looked around the group. "I don't want to jump the gun and promote panic."

"My suggestion," Secretary Goughenbaugh said, "is that we hold off. Although we are sure of the diagnosis, we should have more cases before going public. Continuing our preparation might be our goal at this time."

"Agreed," the trio of physicians said together.

"It's only a guess right now," Dr. Trench went on, "but it seems accurate from what little we've seen of this disease that a significant impact is to be expected among our older population. Particularly those in nursing homes and perhaps even in retirement communities."

"I sent you all a copy of the announcement my Communications people have proposed," Porter said. "Any comments?"

"It seems quite adequate," Dr. Trench said. "Not fomenting panic but advising a cautious and serious approach to whatever comes — that's the right approach."

Porter said, "We are ready to pull the trigger with this and a packet of the material you suggested for the media. I will await word from you, Dr. Talmage." The President looked at his HHS Secretary, saying, "That all right with you, Talmage?"

"Yes, Sir. I'm following the doctors' lead on this."

THE IMPEACHED PRESIDENT

Porter scheduled his Cabinet Meetings on Wednesday mornings. Although some presidents preferred to begin their weeks with these gatherings, Porter knew this would require cabinet staff to work over the weekends to prepare. Thus, he held his meeting on "hump days."

The media was in the Cabinet Room with the seated Cabinet heads before the meeting began asking questions and getting footage for later newscasts. Once the media were herded out, only the President and the Cabinet's staff members were left surrounding the massive table with additional staff seated against the walls. Porter took a brief report from each department secretary and addressed other routine matters on his agenda.

When the meeting broke up two hours later, several officials lingered a moment to get a private word with Porter. One of those hanging back was Secretary of Defense Victor Chesterfield. The bald winner of the Congressional Medal of Honor wore rimless spectacles and clinched an unlit pipe in one hand.

Porter had charged Chesterfield to take over the head of Defense National Intelligence office when the 'grand ol' spy,' Clancy Darren was fired. Within two weeks, Victor had the name of a person to take over the job so Chesterfield could focus his full time attention on being Secretary of Defense. Porter agreed and installed a new Director of DNI.

When Chesterfield took the President's offered hand, he leaned in and quietly said, "When you're alone, check your coat pockets."

Then the mysterious man Porter respected was gone with the other officials.

Porter stood in the private toilet just off the Oval Office. He discovered a folded slip of paper in his right-hand outside coat pocket. He opened the paper and read the hand-printed note: "PEOC Fri. 3

PM." At the bottom of the sheet were the words, "Flash paper. Burn & flush."

The PEOC was the Presidential Emergency Operations Center, over 200 feet underground of the White House. It is the place some thought of as the War Room. The fortified and isolated site was accessible from three different locations in the White House above. Additionally, secret tunnels from other directions could reach the sequestered space, including the Pentagon. Unique stairs and an elevator were located behind hidden panels in the Oval Office and in the Presidential Study.

Porter felt the grit on one half of the sheet of paper he held in his hand. He stood over the toilet, folded the note back in half, then rubbed both sides together between his fingers and his thumb. The paper ignited in a flash, and only a tiny bit of ash remained to drift down into the toilet bowl. Porter watched it drop and then flushed the toilet.

The first lady was late Friday afternoon, returning from her office in the East Wing Presidential Residence. She had been in meetings with Gold Star Mothers about projects they were working on. She arrived at the top of the grand staircase to find Secret Service Joe Lamb and Lt. Col. Alan Coughlin with the "football" briefcase beside his chair. The two were on duty in the hallways running from the East Sitting Hall to the left and the presidential residence to the right.

"Joe, Colonel," Deidra said.

"Ma'am," both men said, getting to their feet.

"The President is already up here?"

"As of several minutes ago," Agent Lamb said.

"Thank you," she said. "Good evening."

"Good evening," they said together.

When Deidra opened the door to the Presidential Bedroom, she removed her heels as she stepped inside the carpeted room.

"Porter," she called, closing the door. Then she saw him. The President was on his knees in front of one of the overstuffed chairs across from their bed. His elbows were on the seat's cushion, his hands folded and his head bowed.

Deidra dropped her shoes and rushed across the room, dropping to her knees beside her husband.

"Porter," she said quietly, understanding that he was praying with his eyes closed.

When he sat back on his heels and opened his eyes, she could see tears running down his cheeks. He took her in his arms.

"What is it?" She gasped.

It took a moment for the President to control his breathing and hug her deeply into his arms. Then, over her shoulder, he said, "This town, our government — the entire world is more corrupt than we could have ever imagined. There is evil rampant in this world which could destroy us all."

CHAPTER 7

In the PEOC, the Presidential Emergency Operations Center, Porter had found Secretary of Defense Victor Chesterfield as he expected. But also in attendance were seven military chiefs of staff from the Army, Navy, Marines, Air Force, Space Force, and National Guard. Conspicuously missing was the Chair and Vice-Chair of the Chiefs of Staff.

The Chair of the Joint Chiefs-of-Staff (JCS) was the principal military adviser to the President, the Secretary of Defense, and the National Security Council. However, all JCS members were by law individual military advisers to the President, the Secretary of Defense, the National Security Council, and the Homeland Security Council. According to the 1986 Goldwater–Nichols Act, none of the Joint Chiefs had operational command authority, either individually or collectively. The chain of command under which they fell went from the President to the Secretary of Defense and from there to the proper combatant commander. There were eleven of these commands: Africa Command (USAFRICOM), Central Command (USCENTCOM), European Command (USEUCOM), Indo-Pacific Command (USIN-DOPACOM), Northern Command (USNORTHCOM), Southern Command (USSOUTHCOM), Space Command (USSPACECOM),

Cyber Command (USCYBERCOM), Special Operations Command (USSOCOM), Strategic Command (USSTRATCOM), and Transportation Command (USTRANSCOM).

The current Chair of the Joint Chiefs was four-star Army General Lee Evans. Evans had seemed to have been an early supporter of Porter — but always in the shadows and behind the scene. He never let his name, rank, nor position become associated with controversial or political decisions regardless of how much the US Armed Forces may have been involved. His absence now concerned the President. Porter returned the salute of those in uniform and took his seat at the head of the long table.

Victor Chesterfield remained standing and took charge of this meeting when all the officers were seated. The widely respected Secretary of Defense was heading this unusual and obliviously clandestine meeting at the PEOC.

"Mr. President," he said, "You will notice the absence of General Evans, his Deputy Chief, and your national Security briefer, Janice Wolff. This is by design. Frankly, we don't believe they can be fully trusted. The Special Access Program we are about to read you into is the most classified operation of our government since the Manhattan project. Please hold your judgment until we are finished."

Victor took a breath, and before he went on. "I once told you that you had no constituency and very little authority as the nation's chief executive. That has all changed with the past election. It is also the opinion of everyone in this room that you are not only President but the chosen person to deal with the profound clear-and-present danger facing our country — and the world. This is not a responsibility you sought, or, I'm sure, one you were even aware existed. And yet, this burden has fallen to you partly by virtue of your office — but more importantly because of your character."

Porter knotted his brow, wondering where all of this was headed.

Chesterfield scanned the faces and saw the nods from every other officer in attendance before continuing.

"Mr. President, you also asked me if you were naïve. I didn't answer that question frankly — but now I can — and I must. You, sir, are indeed naïve — but so is most of the world. And that is by design as well. There are people working very hard, and there are millions of dollars being spent to keep it that way.

"What we are here to explain to you, Mr. President, are the facts as they exist — and the world as it truly exists. This will not be an easy conversation for you or us — but we feel it is one that must be had — and at this time. It is called Project Odin — or The World Reset.

"To begin with, the so-called Deep State is neither a myth nor a conspiracy theory. It is real and a great deal more than a disorganized assortment of petty DC bureaucrats. They are a powerful force of evil — bent on taking over the whole world. We here have known about it for some time and have built a counterinsurgency unlike anything ever imagined.

"The reason we're telling you about this now is because of the upcoming G-7 meeting in London. Your participation in Project Odin — and your leadership — moral and physical — are a must if we are to preserve the world as most people believe it to be. This has not been undertaken lightly by anyone of us nor any of those involved. None of us seek power, position, or remuneration of any kind. What we have begun is an act of patriotism at the very least but hopefully one for all humankind — above and beyond everything else."

"I'm not President of the United States," Porter told Deidra as the two sat on the floor of their bedroom in the East Wing of the White House.

"Of course you are," she said, narrowing her eyes and cocking her head slightly. "I was there when you were sworn in this time." How could he not understand this? Had her husband -- the President -- had a stroke or something?

"It was all for show. I am really the president of the United States of America Corporation. Not a republic. Not a sovereign nation."

"Porter, you're not making any sense."

"I know. I know," he said, wiping his face with his handkerchief.

"We went bankrupt as of the first of July, 1775. Our treasury was empty. We had no money -- nothing. That was when our government discovered there was only one way to obtain the financing we had to have. The answer was to turn our country into a corporation — a corporation that could borrow money to pay our Revolutionary War debts — and our other national obligations. So Congress and our President signed off on the formation of The United States of America *Corporation*. The United States Corporation was chartered in perpetuity in Florida. From that point on, we've been presided over by the British Monarchy, the Vatican, and Rothchild banks. Our Constitution is not the law of the land. We live under corporation statutes. Every Post Office is a British outpost. It oversees all US shipping and commerce. The CIA, FBI, IRS — DNI, NIH — oh, it runs so deep and so wide... I was told to share this with you because Victor and the generals understood how difficult this is to grasp?"

"Victor told you this? Generals and Admirals? I still don't understand, Porter."

"It will take a while to understand — and maybe longer to believe. But, Deidra, we are living in the days the Bible warned us of. We are in the fight of good over evil — such depraved and despicable evil you won't want to believe it. But when you do — it will almost crush you." He paused for a moment. "God gave us each other," slowly pulling her to him. "It's only with His help and guidance that we can withstand this — and hopefully alter the direction of our whole world."

They sat back and looked at each other before Porter went on.

"We went bankrupt a second time after the Civil War. And a third time in 1929 with the Wall Street Crash and the Great Depression. On behalf of a private bank we know as The Federal Reserve, President Roosevelt confiscated the gold of every American citizen. He gave it to that private bank. It is the Federal Reserve that issues notes and coins.

Porter pulled out his wallet and showed Deidra a ten and a twenty dollar bill. "See," he said pointing to the top face of both, "FEDERAL RESERVE NOTE. Jefferson warned us. He told us how a private central banking cartel could get control of the people and the assets of the United States. And they have.

"Both Rothchilds — and now the Rockafellers, too — own the

International Monetary Fund, and the World Bank. They held our debt until November of 1999. At that point, it was the end of a 70-year moratorium period on international bankruptcies. Why haven't they foreclosed? I don't know. I do know that the IRS is a Puerto Rican incorporated Trust — not an agency of the US government.

"And that's just the tip of the iceberg. We've been living on borrowed time. When this second extension ends, we end."

"What does all that mean?"

"It means the Deep State — and New World Order. Those aren't conspiracies. They're real. And there is a backstory to all of it — and a history of unspeakable evil."

He motioned to the bed. There a two-inch-thick manila folder lay wrapped horizontally and vertically in red Velcroed ribbons. Stamped diagonally across the folder in two-inch high embossed letters which read, "Ultra-K Clearance — EYES ONLY." A small fingerprint reader secured the folder.

"All the dirty secrets, all the deceptions, all the lies we have all lived by are explained in there." He sighed and added, "And there is a bigger issue than just this."

"Bigger?" she asked.

"The world — the whole damn world — damned if we don't do our part."

"Are you supposed to have it up here?" the First Lady asked.

"I was told that, unknown to both of us, we have 'Ultra-K' clearance. I didn't know such a clearance level existed. When we're not reading it, we're supposed to keep it in our bedside safe. And we have to read it, Deidra. Because there exists a plan to save the country — and the world. It's called Operation Odin. Like it or not, we are a part of it — and it's win or die."

CHAPTER 8

Hours earlier in the Presidential Emergency Operations Center, Secretary of Defense Victor Chesterfield and the officers explained there was much more to this project and to the evil behind it.

"The so-called New World Order is the goal of the elites and those who believe they rule the earth — and do so by right of wealth, power, and the very evil they embody. It is not only what they have done and want to do to America — they want to kill off millions around the world — change the human race into transhumans' slaves. And we have yet to discuss the source of their money — sex trafficking of children — of women and boys — human beings. They use torture and blood sacrifices. They are ravaging governments and nations with complete corruption. Their agendas can only be called malevolent.

"Our goal — Project Odin — is to disrupt, dismantle and destroy what has become cancerous — devouring — and demonic. It involves what are known as DUMBS — deep underground military bases and structures — and tunnels.

"Some of the major elements of the backstory to all of this are in that folder before you, Mr. President. Share it only with Mrs. Randle

— and no one else. It has been coded to both of your fingerprints. There will be others you'll have to bring in, but please, Sir, only after we've cleared them, Mr. President."

"Then please clear my chief-of-staff and what members of the cabinet you can," Porter said.

"We are on it, Mr. President," Victor said. "I expect Graham Newcome by tomorrow morning. Your Secretaries of State and Treasury are already cleared."

"The time has come, Mr. President," Admiral McCoy Zentmyer said, getting to his feet. He was a tall man, over 6 foot 6, with broad shoulders, a straight nose, and a buzzed cut of the remaining black hair around the edge of his head. He was a natural leader who exuded confidence and authority without even having to try. "The World Reset. The plan is in place — a thorough and detailed plan. You'll find an introduction to it in the folder in front of you. It is a plan conceived by some of the best minds in this country and around the world. Many have been working for years — some for all of their adult life. Some who did not live to see this come to fruition — but they lived and worked in hopes for future generations. These people will never be known, nor their contribution acknowledged. For this project to succeed, we need — not a figurehead – but a true leader. We need you, Mr. President. We need you to step up and take the lead on it — for us — and for the world. All of us in this room believe you are the only man for the job — without question. With respect, Sir, we are not here to ask your permission — nor to seek your participation — but to demand it for the sake of our country — and the world. We need your leadership. We believe your life has led you to this point. That this is your destiny, Sir, just as it is ours. Mr. President, we are here to tell you that — *now is the time, and you are the man.*"

The room was quiet for several moments as Admiral Zentmyer sat. All eyes were focused on Porter. He didn't know what to say at that exact moment. He was overwhelmed.

General Annetta Edsel, stood. Her silver hair framed her face. "Mr. President, we have each had to deal with this — this revelation. And it hit us just as we expect it is striking you. None of us, however, are in a position to do anything but our duty," the four-star Chair of Space Force said. The fit and leggy woman wore bifocals hung on a chain around her neck.

She paused and switched gears saying, "And in that vain we can't emphasize enough how important it is for you to maintain your public demeanor. Your sense of humor, your plain spokenness — all need to remain in full display. The trust the nation and the world had in you must remain in place."

Defense Secretary Victor Chesterfield took the reins of the meeting, saying, "This is especially true, Mr. President, on your weekly podcasts — and when you go to the G-20 meeting next week."

Porter was able to nod his head in understanding, although it was more of a reflex than a considered response. Then, finally, he began to feel the weight of what he knew he was now facing.

"We will be supplying you with evidence on DVDs and in hard copy for your private meeting with specific world leaders," the Secretary of Defense said. "Each will contain some of the information in the folder we've give you, Sir. We understand this is difficult to digest. That's why we've included the First Lady in the clearance for Odin." Victor Chesterfield picked up a cell phone that was on the table before him. He offered it to the President. "This is a special limited encrypted phone, Mr. President. It has the numbers for everyone in this room. When you have questions, please use it exclusively."

Victor Chesterfield took his seat. Porter took a slow deep breath in the silent secure room. He looked at the cell phone and pocketed it. When he finally spoke he said, "First — thank you all for your courage to assume what I can already tell is a giagantic burden — personally — professionally — and patrioticly. Then, what the little I understand of this already I am humbled and honored — to be trusted to be involved with you. I will gladly hang with you if it ever comes to that. Please add my signature as John Handcock did to the Declaration of Independence to Project Odin. My faith and trust in each of you is as deep as yours must be in me. I will do my part — have no doubt about it. I will now go and begin to study and grasp what you have told me and what I've yet to read."

All the officers and the Defense Secretary got to their feet. The officers snapping salutes as if they were choreographed. Porter picked up the folder, stood, returned the salutes, and left.

CHAPTER 9

"Defund The Police!" The new slogan was from protesters/rioters following another police-involved killing of a black man. This time it happened in Kokomo, Indiana. A domestic disturbance call brought two blue and white squad cars to a mostly welfare-supported apartment building. The 911 caller, another resident of the complex, claimed Thiago Hall was once again abusing his ex-wife, Kalina Harris Hall.

When the officer's arrived, they encountered a bloody, beaten, and crying woman of 18 crawling on the sidewalk towards an SUV at the curb. A muscular 20-year-old back man in a wifebeater white t-shirt was pushing two black children into the backseat and carrying a third child in his arms. His hair was cut in what was called a low fade Frohawk — the hair slowly being cut closer and closer to his head and neck as it descended from a high Mohawk running the center length of his skull.

"He's stealin' my kids!" the woman screamed through a bloody mouth with missing teeth.

The police male officers, two black and two white, acted. One black and one white officer went to the mother while the other pair pulled their weapons and took up positions at the front and rear fenders of the SUV. These officers demanded that Thiago Hall put down the child and get on his knees. All of the children were in tears and shrieking incomprehensibly.

Again the officers ordered Thiago Hall to put down the child and get on his knees.

"Can't you see I's got my baby here?" Thiago yelled as he leaned over into the vehicle and put the child he was carrying into a child's seat in the rear.

The officer at the front fender, a white rookie at the end of his first year on the force, had never drawn his weapon before. He had to move into the grass as Thiago was blocked by the open back door of the vehicle.

Once the father had belted the hysterical child into the car seat, he turned right toward the black officer at the back fender. As he moved, he grabbed his 9mm Sig Sauer P226 from the waist of his faded jeans.

"Gun," Sergeant J.B. Davis called, raising his 15 round Beretta 92F.

Before Thiago could get his pistol in firing position, Seargent Davis fired three quick shots into Thiago Hall's chest — killing him instantly. Hall slammed into the back of the open SUV door and dropped to the curb — his weapon ending up under the car.

The protest that night in downtown Kokomo quickly evolved into a raging mob. Professionally printed signs stapled to wooden handles proclaimed "Justice for Thiago," "Black Lives Matter," and "Defund The Police."

The last cabinet position to be filled was the Secretary of the Interior. Ella Suzuki and Ward Adair were Porter's campaign managers in the election. Now they were the two trying to fill all the appointed positions in the administration.

The little-understood office of the Secretary of Interior was created to assist farm families in the permanent settlement of the western US. These days the office focused on conserving and managing federally owned lands. This included several government services ranging from the Bureau of Indian Affairs to the National Parks Service. Because the Secretary of the Interior oversaw an extensive and diverse government department, the position could have some very unique demands.

The person in this position must coordinate federal policy in the territories of American Samoa, Guam, the US Virgin Islands, and the Commonwealth of the Northern Mariana Islands. Additionally, the Secretary of the Interior had to administer and oversee US federal assistance provided to the Freely Associated States of the Federated States of Micronesia, the Republic of the Marshall Islands, and the Republic of Palau under the Compacts of Free Association.

As a member of the Presidential Cabinet, they were in line for the succession of the Presidency — eighth in line. The Secretary of the Interior must be confirmed in the Senate before taking office.

The Department of the Interior ran numerous agencies. They included the Bureau of Land Management (BLM), the Bureau of Reclamation (BR), the US Geological Survey (USGS), the Office of Surface Mining (OSM), and the United States Fish and Wildlife Service (USFWS). In their own way, each was responsible for protecting federal lands and ensuring that they were used in sustainable and beneficial practices. Additionally, the Secretary had mandates that include directives to ensure that all Americans access federally owned lands. This ranged from the nation's National Parks to the open stretches of land in the American West, leased to cattle ranchers.

Typically the holder of this office was someone from the American West. It was someone who had lived with and under the decisions of previous holders of the office.

In her usual good-humored way, Forty-three-year-old Ella Suzuki had nudged her husband into dealing with this office as late as possible. While technically being a westerner, she was from California and a city girl. Husband Ward Adair, who was known to be intense and blunt, grew up in suburban Columbus, Ohio.

Their list of possible candidates for the Interior position focused on rancher and cattleman Linton Ston. He had turned his holdings into an expansive company he now managed as a corporation in Boise, Idaho.

"I'm an environmentalist who doesn't buy the Climate Change bull shit," the beefy and bowlegged rancher said, "any more than I did the whole Green New Deal swindle." Ston came to DC at Ward's request and now sat across from him and his wife in their Eisenhauser Executive Office building suite. "I'm not a tree hugger, but I have more respect for the earth than any face painted, sign-holding, son of a bitch who has ever worked the land a day in their sheltered life," said the even 6 foot, taut figure wearing creased jeans, a fringed buckskin jacket, with a Western string tie held together with turquoise, mother-of-pearl, and onyx Native American medallion. "Poisoning the land, water, and the air is what I'm against. And none of it is caused by cow farts. I want you to know that up front. If that strikes me from your list, let's not waste each other's time."

"Not at all," Ella said. "The President is looking for someone with more common sense than protest experience."

"You have worked with the BLM," Ward said, "and you understand how they work with people who actually work the land."

"I trust you're talking about The Bureau of Land Management and not Black Lives Matter?" Ston asked seriously.

"Of course," Ella said. "It's one of the agencies the Secretary of the Interior oversees."

"Then, yes, I have. I've also had dealings with some knuckleheads in the Bureau of Reclamation, the Geological Survey, the Office of Surface Mining, and the Fish and Wildlife Service. There are too many bureaucrats and not enough real people running those offices. They don't understand how those of us who work the soil take care of it."

"As Secretary of the Interior, you would be able to change that — and do it with the President's support," Ward said. He and Ella exchanged looks, and then Ward said, "We'd like to submit your name to the President — if you're game."

Ston uncrossed his legs and put both cowboy boots on the Parkey floor as he leaned forward. He said, "I'd be honored."

"A couple of things the President would like for you to do," Ella said. "Clean house and get the deadwood off the payroll. Then tackle the regulations."

"And do what with them?" Ston wanted to know.

"Eighty-six those that are no longer needed," Ward said, "and prune the ones that are left but which have gone too far. You've lived under them and will have a better sense of which have gone too far and which are just bullshit from page one."

"That," Linton Ston said, "I would gladly undertake."

CHAPTER 10

"What is the Galactic Federation? And what non-humanoids — extra-terrestrial — are in existence on the surface of Earth — and throughout our shared galaxy?" the President asked.

"One moment, please," the Secretary of Defense said into his encrypted phone.

Porter heard Victor Chesterfield say, "We'll have to pick this up later."

Several voices said, "Yes, sir."

There were a few moments of silence and the sound of a closing door heard by Porter. Then he heard Victor say, "Mrs. Elam, hold my calls." A female voice from an intercom said, "Yes, sir. Holding your calls."

Back into the cell phone, the Secretary of Defense said, "The Galactic Federation of Light. I know it sounds very Twilight Zone, but it's for real. We have Galactic Brothers and Sisters of the Light who are planning for a major landing on the surface of Earth — what they call Gaia. They will be led by a spiritually-advanced race of beings known as the Pleiadians.

"We will join 'The Galactic Federation of Light,' Mr. President, when we can prove ourselves worthy. We will live among other off-world races. We will trade with them and travel to other planets inhabited by humanoid alien races. It's all part of a secret space program we've been running for decades. That's why we have a Space Force, Sir."

"This is a lot to take in," Porter said.

"I know. You haven't gotten down to the papers in the folder we gave you and the First Lady, which explains all of this."

"No, we haven't. I'm in my study studying the GESARA and NESARA for the G-20 meeting."

"I understand. The Pleiadians look very similar to the human race. And, I think that's the big reason they have been chosen to lead the advance team – because of their human-looking features — to keep us from freaking out."

"Makes sense," Porter said with a sigh. "I keep thinking I'm going to wake up any moment now, and I'm back in Texas and still a practicing surgeon."

"Trust me, Sir, we all felt that way when we first became aware of all of this. It sounds as if we've taken LSD or have gone squirly in the head. But it's real — and we need to discuss this in-depth."

"Agreed. I'll keep studying here as will Deidra and I together with the other material."

"I'm glad you used this phone, Mr. President. And feel free to whenever you have a need."

"Thank you, Victor." Porter took a breath and said, "Let me shift gears. All this rioting has me worried. Where do we stand with "posse comitatus?"

"Well, Sir, The Posse Comitatus Act dates to 1878, the end of Reconstruction. It helped return white supremacists to political power in southern states and Congress. Democrats, in power then, sought through the law to ensure that the federal military would not be used to intervene in the establishment of Jim Crow in the former Confederacy."

Porter could hear Victor tapping his teeth with the stem of his unlit pipe as he thought and spoke.

"The broader principle was that the military should not be allowed to interfere in the affairs of civilian government."

As Porter took all of this in, Victor seemed to pause a few moments.

When the Secretary of Defense continued, he said, "When operating under Title 32, however, the National Guard forces are exempt from the Posse Comitatus — because they are under state command and control. A key part of that control is the governor's right to decline a particular federal mission. A cooperating governor could become a fig leaf for the president to use the military as police anywhere in the country, free from the posse comitatus constraints. If, on the other hand, the president approaches a difficult governor and asks them to deploy the state's Guard and the governor refuses — the president is stuck."

"Are there no constitutional exceptions?"

"The law allows only for express exceptions, and no part of the Constitution expressly empowers the president to use the military to execute the law. However, it hasn't stopped the DoD from claiming that constitutional exceptions do exist. For example, the Department has long held that the Constitution implicitly gives military commanders' emergency authority' to unilaterally use federal troops 'to quell large-scale, unexpected civil disturbances.' Like when Hoover used the troops to clear the Bonus Army from DC campsites. Or Ike, who used the National Guard to implement segregation in Little Rock, Arkansas, in 1957. In other words, when doing so is 'necessary' and prior authorization from Congress is impossible — say due to time or particular circumstances. Then the president can act. The DoD has also claimed an inherent constitutional power to use the military to protect federal property — or when local governments could not or would not do so. However, the validity of these claimed authorities has never been tested in court.

"Now, The Insurrection Act is a statutory exception to the Posse Comitatus Act, Mr. President. Under this law, in response to a state government's request, the president may deploy the military to suppress an insurrection in that state. In addition, the Insurrection Act allows the president — with or without the state government's consent

— to use the military to enforce federal law or suppress a rebellion against federal authority in a state — or to protect a group of people's civil rights when the state government is unable or unwilling to do so."

"Thank you, Victor," Porter said. "This is what we may have to use against these rioters. Unfortunately, neither the local nor the state officials seem willing to do what needs to be done."

"You're talking about that ANTIFA bunch in particular?"

"Them, the BLM, and those they seem to empower."

"I'll have my people begin looking into that. Then, we'll be ready to move if you need us — even while you're overseas."

"Thank you. I couldn't ask for more. Thank you, Mr. Secretary."

"At your service, Mr. President.

CHAPTER 11

"You know I hate you, don't you? And I'll never forgive you for talking me into this."

Dexter Fetterman, Secretary of State, shook hands at the door to the Oval Office with Porter. The 55-year-old, dark-skinned, portly, and slightly nasal-voiced man with close trimmed white-bearded and high forehead added his left hand warmly, greeting the President on top of his right despite his words. When he read, the 6 foot 3-inch official wore half-glasses on the end of his broad nose but usually kept them on a black anodized stainless steel chain.

"I have a cheese plate and some crackers and meat to go with that whine," Porter smiled as Fetterman stepped in and the President closed the door.

"Oh, good," Fetterman said, headed for a seat on one couch where Graham Newcome stood, awaiting the two-time Pulitzer Prize-winning, four-time National Book Award-winning non-fiction author.

"Dr. Fetterman," Graham smiled as he offered his hand.

"Graham," the Secretary said, shaking hands with the President's Chief-of-Staff. He parked his briefcase on one of the couch cushions before taking a cracker in hand and covering it with Brie.

Porter took his seat across from both men smiling. He pointed out the three mini silver serving dishes on the meat and cheese platter. "There is some tangy cheddar and Limburger if you prefer."

Finishing his first bite, Fetterman said, "So, the plan is to keep my mouth full and shut, is it?"

Laughing, Porter said, "Not at all. But these are specially prepared for you, Dexter."

The Secretary finished his first cracker before he spoke. "You know, I could be home in Connecticut — with a fireplace and my dogs — writing about all the things this administration is getting wrong on the international stage — instead of being here and up to my neck waddle engineering part of it."

"A dozen books on US foreign policy. Pro and con," Porter said with a twinkle in his eye. "Well, mostly con. Bestsellers all. You exposed how *not* to make state policy. We both know you were more knowledgeable about how it should be done than anyone who has ever had the title and authority of Secretary of State. Naturally, I thought it was a chance for you to practice what you sermonized about. Now a Nobel literature nomination isn't enough? You want the whole thing?" Porter joked.

"I'll get it when I get back to my computer, and all of this is history."

"Wouldn't doubt it for a second," Porter smiled. "But for the moment, you're still Secretary of State, and we have a G-20 to attend."

"Okay, okay," Fetterman said, opening his briefcase beside him and extracting a folder.

Graham picked up a pale blue legal pad from the end of the coffee table and got out a ballpoint from an inside coat pocket to make notes.

"What are your concerns?" Porter asked.

"That some of the countries we — make that 'you' — will be trying to get onboard will think our interest is more in NESARA than GESARA. The worldwide corporation will not be easy to achieve among nations who have never trusted nor agreed with others on anything. So now we're trying to get them to invest themselves in a universal financial switch that will only work if it works everywhere."

"Good worry," Porter said. "But I've already discussed this with Secretary Speering." Leola Speering was the Secretary of the Treasury.

The former head of a computer corporation and then a major US-based international bank CEO. "I believe we will have fewer problems there due to the global potential of this new China virus."

"China virus? Are you actually going to use that phrase?"

"To everyone except China," the President said. "But even China knows what they're not saying and what the truth is."

"You understand the world is going to look to us for treatments, and a possible cure, don't you?"

"Yes. But it is way too early in that game to begin to expect much. Talmage Goughenbaugh is even worried — and the best people in the world are in his HHS."

"I damn sure hope so," Fetterman reached for another cracker and sampled the cheddar with a slice of salami. "And they are also going to be watching what we're doing about all these 'peaceful protests.'"

"I'm working on that," Porter said.

"We have to stay within the bounds of posse comitatus," Graham added.

"It's too early to take that direction," Porter said. "But Victor Chesterfield is aware we may have to -- and has his people studying it."

"Studying — writing — ah, those were the days. Don't you miss your fiction, Porter?"

"I do — and I dabble with notions and make notes a lot — but for both of us, it's neither the season nor the time for such things."

"Agreed — reluctantly, I want to say — on the record."

"Noted," Porter said. "I was wondering if you wanted to go with me to London or take your plane?"

"In spite of concerns of the environment and much to the left's delight, I am taking my plane along with Leola and much of her staff. She's not taking her plane, and since I don't need my whole carrol, we thought we'd go together."

"Excellent," Porter said.

The Secretary sampled the cracker with the cheddar with an approving smile. "I'm avoiding the Limburger for the sake of everyone I'll encounter this afternoon. But, oh, the sacrifices we make for the country."

Porter and Graham laughed.

"Anything, in particular, we need to go over?" Porter asked. "We're on the same page with Afghanistan — so what else is there that you're involved in, Dexter?"

When the Secretary could speak again, Fetterman looked through the folder in his lap before he said, "We're getting hard pushback from China over the Wuhan flight cancellations."

"I expected that. It will be face-saving on the part of the Chinese — but I'm not willing to keep an open road for them to continue to funnel carriers of this virus right into here."

"They will just use other routes, take other flights, you know."

"I'm sure, but we have no way of checking the origin of every person aboard every flight."

"We would if you'd let the CIA have their way."

"And none of us wants that, now, do we?" the President said with a sarcastic tone.

"No, Sir, we don't," the Secretary said, shaking his head. "Are we going to cut off any funds on this trip or simply announce our intent?"

"I look at this as our shot across the bow. Let's see what happens — particularly with NATO. I have a conference with them in Brussels this summer."

"This could be a long hot summer, Mr. President."

"Yes, it could — and I'm getting ready to apply some heat from here if needed."

"I may be asking you to accumulate some big-time air miles."

"I knew that was going to be part of this job."

CHAPTER 12

The same day as the shooting occurred in Indiana, the WHO, the World Health Organization, announced a mysterious Coronavirus-related pneumonia had been discovered in Wuhan, China. It was not known whether or not the virus developed in wildlife populations.

Before the Kokomo riots erupted that night and were being carried live by multiple cable TV channels, the White House Press Office issued the statement it had prepared about COVID. The message stated that the US National Institute of Health was aware of the virus and was tracking it. The case of the sales agent in Seattle was noted. Additionally, they pointed out the fact that the patient fully recovered.

The next afternoon Porter took Vice President Holyoak along with NIH Director Dr. Judson Whitehead, Dr. Sinead Trench, and Dr. Laurennie Jarry into a surprised White House Press Room. Porter made a brief statement and announced the closing of all flights to and from Wuhan, China. Next, he was joined at the podium by the Vice President.

Tracy Holyoak, her hazel eyes flashing, introduced herself as the Covid Task Force leader Porter had appointed for what was the disease that had the potential to be a pandemic. The 4 foot, 11-inch ash-blonde VP projected confidence and a grasp of the situation. She, in turn, presented the medical and administrative experts who were there to explain the new disease as it was currently understood.

Dr. Sinead Trench, Director of the National Institute of Allergies and Infectious Diseases, and Dr. Laurennie Jarry, Director of National Institute of Biomedical Imaging and Bioengineering, stepped up. The pair shared the podium as reporters began their exciting queries.

Porter and Tracy stepped down from the platform when the questioning was well underway. The Vice President remained, but Porter exited the briefing. In suspenders and a button-down collared shirt, Howard Sterling sat in a chair beside the riser to oversee the media questioning with the Vice President.

Back in the Presidential Study off the Oval Office, Porter continued the prep for the G-20 meeting in five days. Firstly, his agenda was his announcement to all members that US aid was not endless. Unless the other G-20 nations began immediately to contribute their financial pledges to the promised projects, the US would start to withhold its share. He also said the same was true for NATO members and their military organization. The yearly obligation here was 0.3% of each member's defense spending. Last, Porter wanted to seek the expected impact of COVID on G-20 nations.

He had a private meeting scheduled with each attending world leader as a part of his duties. Examining the material for the United Kingdom in his private study, he began to familiarize himself with the major obstacles. GESARA (Global Economic Security And Reformation Act) had some obstacles. The President's charge was to have each participating nation to quietly and legislatively pass this act as a NESARA (National Economic Security And Reformation Act). It was already secretly accomplished in the US.

The act would require the elimination of the International Monetary Fund (IMF) and The World Bank and a complete realignment of the World Trade Organization (WTO). Other primary tenants of this move would be a proclamation of a global jubilee or debt forgiveness and the universal reset of planetary currency. The new system was to be twofold. First, a universal system of shared governance. Second, switching to a Quantum Financial System. Precious metals backed this system (gold, silver, and platinum). The entire purpose was to achieve good transparent standing with other 'member beings of the Galactic Federation.'

The end game was to have 209 sovereign nations, all of which signed the 2015 Paris Agreement on Climate Change, implement and began serving under a universal constitutional framework for global governance. It was, to start with, the restored Republic of the United States.

It also entailed the mass disclosure of non-humanoid (extra-terrestrial) life in existence on the surface of Earth and throughout our shared galaxy.

This was the point at which Porter fished his newly acquired encrypted cell phone from his pocket and selected the Secretary of Defense's number.

Porter spent two hours on the phone arranging for his own panel of advisors on the China virus. Using a unique encrypted Zoom app on the computer in his study, he first sought advice from friends, then former military colleagues, even his general family practice physician daughter in Lubbock. Next, he accumulated a group of widely published and respected virus and infectious disease specialists. Porter made sure his list did not include any who had already been tapped for Vice President Holyoak's Task Force. After talking to several who were available, he narrowed his list to three.

In the end, he got all three on a Zoom call and introduced each to the others. While each had heard of these colleagues, only two had ever had any contact — and that was at medical conferences over the years. Satisfied with his choices, Porter told them they would receive visits from the Secret Service. The agents would either encrypt a special Zoom app on their current computers or provide them with an already encrypted device for their future contacts with the President.

Porter explained he wanted their independent opinions on COVID-related matters, past and present — even if they didn't agree with each other. While Porter was an MD, he explained his specialty was surgery. And even though he knew some about epidemics and pandemics, they would have to make sure he understood their ideas.

Briefly, on this initial call, the group explained that the SARS-CoV-2 strain causes COVID. Meaning it is a novel strain of the Betacoronavirus. An earlier strain was responsible for the 2003 SARS-CoV-1 and the 2009 Middle East Respiratory Syndrome Coronavirus, known as MERS. The genomes of SARS stood for Acute Respiratory Syndrome. As these doctors currently understood it, the SARS-CoV-2 was the one the WHO had announced in China.

They explained SARS is a viral respiratory illness caused by a coronavirus. It was first reported in Asia in February 2003. The sickness spread over the next few months to over two dozen countries in North America, South America, Europe, and Asia before the global outbreak of '03 was contained.

According to the World Health Organization, 8,098 people worldwide became sick with the virus during the 2003 outbreak. Of these, 774 died.

In the states, only eight people had laboratory evidence of SARS infection. All of these people had traveled to other parts of the world where the virus was spreading at the time. Although governmental officials feared an outbreak, it did not spread widely in the US.

Close contact was identified as the means of transmission. This included having cared for or lived with someone with SARS or having direct contact with respiratory secretions or body fluids of a patient with the disease. Other examples of close contact included kissing or hugging, sharing eating or drinking utensils, talking to someone within 3 feet, and touching someone directly. However, one doctor said that close contact did not include walking by a person or briefly sitting across an office or waiting room from others.

Prescribed prevention involved physical distancing, mask-wearing, hand hygiene, and staying away from others if you feel sick.

Porter thanked them for their insights and said he would ensure all three received samples of the isolated pathogens and genome as soon as available. He then told them to expect a telephone call from his personal secretary for payroll information. They would be Special Advisors to the President and be reimbursed accordingly. The President also warned them to keep this association quiet for the moment, or they would become hounded by the media for inside scoops on anything known or suspected. He explained political lines would be drawn like most topics in the nation's capital, and science and truth would be the first victims. And, if any ideas they might have that might later prove erroneous, regardless of intent, their observations could be used as a cudgel against them individually later.

They understood, and while they declined the need for pay, the President insisted they were acting as professional consults and should be regarded as such.

The three physicians understood and were even thankful for the honor of advising the President. Porter, however, reminded them he did not want them ever to tell him what they might believe he wanted to hear but to offer their best advice — even if it seemed in complete opposition to the thinking of WHO or that of the NIH.

CHAPTER 13

Porter's last Saturday podcast before he left for the G-20 was all about dreams and race.

His laptop was open on a lamp table in front of the fireplace in the Oval Office. The President was dressed in a gray turtleneck sweater and black slacks.

He said over the internet, "We're now in Black History month. Down the years, the voice of Dr. Martin Luther King, Jr., echoes to us — 'I have a dream.' We know his dream of equality, justice for all, and peace.

"Dr. King is remembered for his dream — his vision of hope, love, and the brotherhood of all humanity — not for his being a victim of an assassin's bullet. His life was more important than his death. It was so with John F. Kennedy, Abraham Lincoln, Mohandas Gandhi, Jimi Hendrix, John Lennon, Robin Williams, Princess Diana, Freddie Prinze, Buddy Holly, Isaac Hayes, Vincent van Gogh, Whitney Houston, Santana, and Ernest Hemingway.

"What will be history's remembrance of you? Are you a victim?

"History primarily remembers victims by their numbers — 6 million jews killed by Hitler, 3,000 killed on 9/11 (although I believe it's more like 8,000+), as well as those who have died in floods, hurricanes, and other natural disasters. We remember the number of victims of tragic events but do we know their names and remember their accomplishments in life?

"What is your dream? Where will you be 10 —20 —30 years from now? Have you accomplished your objectives — are you making progress towards them? It's never too late. Grandma Moses didn't start painting until she was 78 years old.

"Anything worthwhile takes time and effort. I know cartoonists like to make fun of my playing the banjo, but how many of them can pick up the instrument and play it at all? I'm aware that Mark Twain famously said, 'A gentleman is someone who knows how to play the banjo and doesn't.' But I take pride and joy from playing this instrument brought to us by enslaved Black people a couple of centuries ago.

"Who are your idols? Who do you look up to? Do they inspire you — or help you believe in your victimhood? Are you proud to be an American or not?

"Writer George M. Haddad once penned these words in a piece entitled 'Who Suffers at the hands of the Race Hustlers?,' He wrote, 'There is no perfect world out there. There is no country on this earth without prejudice. But some … living in the greatest and most generous country, this globe has ever spawned, … reek of despair. They have been blessed to live in a nation where millions of people throughout this world would give everything they own to live (here) and not without good reason.'

"This month is one often exploited by race hustlers. Who are they? Professional race hustlers or race haters are people who promote division and fear. They exploit racial and ethnic tensions to advance personal, political, ideological, or financial agendas. Follow the money. Do any of the race haters, and I don't need to name them — we all know who they are — do any of them live in your neighborhood, live the way you live? They are the ones who always show up at any opportunity to spew their identity politics — collect funds on behalf of the cause of the moment — and then return to their lifestyle — way above and beyond that of those they claim to represent — with all or a piece of the donated and collected currency.

"Clarence Page, the journalist, syndicated columnist, and senior member of the Chicago Tribune editorial board, wrote that '...the myopic focus on the oppression of black people is depriving them of agency. It degrades and casts aside the great accomplishments of what he calls black overcoming.'

"The race hustler's dream and ongoing narrative *is* racial division — victimhood — even a racial war. And for them, it's all about the benjamin's — getting their cut of the Ghetto Lottery from the poor and the suffering.

"Their tactics are to make everything about race. Forget history — except for the warped history they want you to buy into. Keep the idea of slavery alive — use the term 'White Privilege' to disarm facts and logic that disrupts our victimhood. Accept no responsibility for your life — it's all the white man's fault. They encourage their audience to make up their facts and repeat them until they are believed. It worked for Hitler and Mao — it'll work again.

'Hispanics, Asians, and other minorities — they don't fit in. Of course, they don't. They would corrupt the narrative — the storyline. Just as the fact that it was the white man who fought and died to end slavery.

"There should be no other dreams, according to these race hustlers, except those they dictate. They tell you to wallow in your victimhood and celebrate your lack of fathers in homes, and abandon religion — but by all means, avoid the culture of achievement and standards. Keep the n-word for yourself in your music and everyday language. Don't allow whitie to use it. Remember spelling, mathematics, attention to detail, punctuality, and cleanliness — those are all white concepts and none of your own. Above all, do not accept any responsibility for your life, decisions, or actions. Don't curse those who take the needle, pills, or bottle. They deserve their piece of oblivion — it is their lot in life because of their race. To struggle against it is to become a willing servant, if not slave, to *the man*."

Here Porter paused a moment. He took a drink of water from a glass on the lamp table. When he continued, he said, "Were the civil rights leaders of the past dupes and failures?

"Is illiteracy your friend?

"Are black people, as Clarence Page wrote, '...helpless bystanders in their own history...'?

"Or do you have a dream? A dream worth struggling for? One worth achieving? An aspiration worth your life? A dream to be remembered by Black History Month in the future?"

"Will you be an Ibram X. Kendi, Al Sharpton, Jesse Jackson, or Louis Farrakhan? Or will you be the George Washington Carver, Frederick Douglass, WEB Du Bois, Maya Angelou, Jesse Owens, Toni Morrison, Nelson Mandela, Martin Luther King, Jr., Dr. Ben Carson, Robert Woodson, Candice Owens, or Thomas Sowell of the future?

"Do you have a dream?"

CHAPTER 14

Again in the PEOC, after the formalities of salutes. Porter sat, as did the others in the room. Defense Secretary Victor Chesterfield remained standing. Porter held up a hand and said, "Before we do anything else, I need to get a better understanding of the Galactic Federation. I feel as if we've slipped into Star Wars Land. Explain this to me in a way I can grasp it without having to put on a tin hat."

General Jovelen Door stood, and the Defense Secretary sat. The 50-year-old woman with golden brown eyes and a clear complexion stood.

Porter said, "Please, sit, General. And everyone else, keep your seats."

General Door sat back down. The 6 foot tall with red/blonde hair cut to military specifications said, "Mr. President, interplanetary space travel is not only possible — it's shared across the universe. We have been in contact with members of The Galactic Federation — the Pleiadians. Technology they have given us is the reason the Space Force even exists today.

"I believe Secretary Chesterfield talked to you briefly about the Pleiadians. Their star system, the Pleiades star system, is some 440 light-years from Earth. The Pleiadians themselves look very similar to humans. They have eyes, nose, mouth, ears, two arms, two legs, and look human. That, I believe, is why the Pleiadians were picked to lead the advanced team we've met with.

"This gets to be — *science fiction* now. Their civilization currently exists in the sixth dimension. They communicate by telepathy, and use anti-gravity propulsion for their spacecraft."

General Annetta Edsel, Chief of Staff of the Army, picked up the bifocals which hung around her neck on a silver chain. She glanced at her notes occasionally while trying to keep eye contact with the President. "They 'ascended' from the lower dimensions to the higher dimensions of consciousness millions of years ago. They've had a similar ascension process as humanity is going through now.

"Contact with earthlings has been kept to a minimum as much as possible to obey the Universal Law of Non-Interference by the Galactic Federation. The first people they contacted already had a genetic link with certain galactic civilizations. These people live a life on Earth on behalf of the Pleiadians — they want to have experiences they can later share.

"Generally, they stay in the background. However, they guarantee that the Ascension process goes as planned and that the actions of the Illuminati be monitored. Those are the people who are trying everything to disrupt this process. And not very effectively. Our alien friends are keeping the oxygen level in our air up to the mark, and they are preventing nuclear attacks. They clean up radioactive fallout that already exists and are eliminating chemical pollution, chemtrails, and diseases. They're also minimizing the effects of natural disasters — artificial or not."

"What man-made natural disasters?" the President asked.

General Denver Kimble, the Chief of Staff of the Air Force, spoke up. He had short brown but receding hair. The 56-year-old officer had a jutting chin and a Roman nose.

"Mr. President, we have HAARP weapons — that's High-Frequency Active Auroral Research Project. Though we officially deny their existence, technologies have been used for weather control. They can cause earthquakes, hurricanes, tsunamis — and disrupt global communications systems. We are cautious in how and where we use these weapons."

The Commandant of the Marine Corps, Four-Star General Knox Welch, said, "About 40% of the Galactic Federation is human. The rest consists of other species and what are called light beings." The beefy and chiseled 55-year-old had a full head of dark hair with a streak of silver from his forehead back. He had a commanding voice that demanded attention. "Since the population on Earth is human, the human civilizations within the Galactic Federation play an essential role in assisting our ascension process. Many of them share a genetic link with us but are more highly developed than we are.

"The Galactic Federation has an enormous fleet of space ships at its disposal that mediate, or if needed, intervene in any place where conflicts impend. The interdimensional technologies they can use are of such a high level we can hardly imagine them. Their control of energy is almost perfect, so things like dematerializing, becoming invisible, or creating small orbs of energy are no problem at all.

"Their ships are often created of living material. The Federation's fleet comprises vessels of the participating worlds and several singly operating fleets.

"At this moment, a considerable part of the Galactic Federation is present around the Earth to bring the tumultuous end of our cycle of duality to a happy conclusion."

General Jovelen Door spoke up once more. The red/blonde-haired general said, "Although our entire universe has ascended — the Ascension of the Earth is different. There are millions of ships that are currently hovering around the Earth. This is no static presence. Ships are continuously arriving and departing — as we evolve."

General Denver Kimble of the Air Force spoke once more.

"They have visited our planet for millions of years and left behind many souvenirs, such as buildings and art objects. However, many of them have been made by hostile alien visitors who are no part of the Galactic Federation.

"This link with extraterrestrials is hidden as much as possible by mainstream science, which is under the control of the Illuminati."

Secretary Chesterfield spoke for the first time.

"The heads of governments on Earth mostly know of their existence. However, their exercise of transparency will change. And it's already begun. New findings all over the planet are evidence of this. According to the changelings we know and have spoken to, they will soon show themselves publicly. And when they do, their superior technology will partially become available for us."

The secure room was silent for a few moments. Porter took all the information in and sighed. "So, is there anything more I need to know — something I need to do?"

"You are doing very well, Mr. President," Victor said. "The Pleiadians do not want to interfere with you or what you do. They seem to feel you are acting in the best interest of the planet, and they don't want that to change."

"So, I just go on as if they are not there?"

"For the moment, Mr. President. If and when that changes, they will let us know."

CHAPTER 15

The G-20 is an expansion of the G7 — once the largest economic club globally. The new kid on the block, the G-20, evolved because more countries needed financial help internationally due to East Asian turmoil in 1999. As a result, a bigger collective was required to respond to the crises.

The G-20 became more than an annual meeting for the world's most prominent economic leaders. Technically, it included 19 countries plus the European Union. Together these nations account for two-thirds of the planet's population and represent 85% of the world's economy. The member states were Argentina, Australia, Brazil, Canada, China, France, Germany, India, Indonesia, Italy, Japan, the Republic of Korea, Mexico, Russia, Saudi Arabia, South Africa, Turkey, the United Kingdom, the United States, and the European Union.

Dealing with the 1999 crisis proved that the G-20 was faster and more adept at handling global financial problems than the UN, the World Bank, or the IMF. Moreover, the 172 other countries who were not invited were, by and large, not made up for a single leader to make significant changes overnight without consulting a congress or parliament. Thus, the Big Boys could do so while sitting around a table without the hassle of the slowly grinding wheels of individual governments.

In order not to be slow to react or having to quickly assemble leaders in the event of an urgent monetary event, the G-20 had adopted a schedule of twice-yearly meetings at the same time as the International Monetary Fund and the World Bank.

Porter had attended the three previous meetings, and he was a known quantity. The few new leaders of other countries had to be made aware that the cortile American was a fair-minded but solid negotiator and not a man to be taken lightly on any topic.

Again this year, the G-20 focused on responding to the terrorist attacks. Both London and Paris had been the latest sites of terrorist bombs. In addition, the growing number of refugees escaping the ISIS war was burdening Italy and other European nations. Further steps to cut off financing for ISIS were also on the table.

Porter's announcement of US withdrawal from Afghanistan was the big story the first day of the meeting. The strict conditions of US withdrawal were outlined, and a warning was issued to the Taliban. Any interference with the US movement of troops would be met with harsh and instantaneous responses.

In the international press conference late the first afternoon, Porter explained that America's longest and costless war was no longer one the US intended to continue. With neither territorial nor mineral ambitions, this was a war the United States had sacrificed too much blood and treasure to achieve too little. He said it was a hard lesson to learn, but "a ground war in Asia" is indeed a foolish entanglement. "Russia had learned the same lesson on the same ground before us," he told the media. "And it's the history we don't read and understand that we repeat. We tried to help the nation of Afghanistan, but nation-building is not an aspiration we wish to pursue. What will become of that country is a topic we will discuss here, but it is primarily up to the villagers and the tribes of the land who have to decide what they want.

"The Americans who lost lives and limbs in that fight," Porter continued, "did so with honor and for what was once believed to be a goal we could and should try to achieve. But in the end, Afghanistan is not a US territory nor a stable ally and might never be. The mindset of the average Afghani differs greatly from those of the average Westerner. It is not ours to tell them our way is right and their way is wrong. As in Vietnam, the people have not risen to support the US fight — so we will no longer attempt to be the policeman of the world nor the savior of it, either."

At home, the media jumped on the fact that the President chose to make his announcement overseas instead of to the American public first. The Randall administration responded that the decision was reached in consultation with allies involved in the conflict. The change in status of US forces was to be accompanied by a similar move by the other nations participating in the war. Therefore, it was only fair that the announcement be made there where those allied with us could react as they wished.

The fact that others in the obstetrically NATO-led UN mission — to train, advise, and assist Afghan troops — all spoke up and agreed with the US did not register with the American media. It was given little more than scant coverage. Instead, Porter was rebuked for "cutting and running in the face of the enemy" — a charge which some speculated to lead to another attempted impeachment.

Porter's side meetings with other world leaders were characterized by their secret and silent agreement with GESARA and NESARA. The world's uber-rich and Illuminati had formed an evil CABAL. This conspiracy had long held the world in a fiat currency system in which countries were forced to print money with nothing behind it.

At gunpoint and surrounded by Special Forces in the US, President

Bill Clinton signed the NESARA bill, National Economic Security and Recovery Act, into law on October 10, 2000. Clinton, however, knew that the CABAL was still in charge and that this law was never to be enforced. NESARA was originally to be implemented on September 11, 2001. However, computers on the second floor of One World Trade Center were destroyed in the attack. These machines contained data of the beneficiaries of the trillions of dollars in "Prosperity Funds." Trillions in recovered gold had also been stored beneath the complex. It all disappeared.

Now GESARA, Global Economic Security and Reformation Act, was to be implemented. It involved the military of the G-7 powerhouses, but also worldwide media takeovers, and a Quantum Financial System, which would be unhackable. In addition, gold and silver were to be captured from the CABAL and repatriated to the countries from which they had been stolen.

Although there was some skepticism, GESARA was ultimately endorsed by all G-20 attendees.

CHAPTER 16

As Porter explained it, "The human race has known since the end of March, 2018, that our 'Galactic Brothers and Sisters of the Light' are now planning for a major landing on the surface of Gaia (Earth). There are people who know this is already in every nation. Seek them out. They aren't all kooks. The first wave of landings will be led by a spiritually advanced race of beings known as the Pleiadians.

"The Pleiadians look very similar to the human race. They come from the Pleiades star systems, approximately 440 light-years from Earth.

"Their entire civilization currently exists in the sixth dimension, while ours is a three-dimensional reality. Pleiadians communicate by telepathy, and use anti-gravity propulsion for their spacecraft. They 'ascended' from the lower dimensions to the higher dimensions of consciousness millions of Earth years ago. They've had a very similar ascension process as humanity and Earth (Gaia) are going through right now.

"GESARA is the ending event of a greater reclaiming for our world. What it's all about is just the opposite of The New World Order. We're calling it The Great Reset."

He explained to each leader what they should expect from GESARA:

1. Money everyone around the world now has in the banks are safe; Financial privacy will be restored; each citizen under the news Quantum Financial System will have their account, and it will remain private, not subject to bank or government oversight;

2. Income for seniors will increase three times current levels;

3. Credit card balances, mortgages, and other declared illegal bank debts would be forgiven;

4. Fiat currency (unbacked printed money) will be replaced with rainbow currency back by tangible precious metals;

5. Income tax in every nation will be abolished, and citizens will be repaid all monies paid under income tax laws since 1948; only sales taxes at a 12-17% rate would fund governments;

6. Within 120 days of "zero-day," (full implementation of GESARA), new fraud-free elections will be held for national leaders and legislatures;

7. Release of new technologies will take place; including 6,000 patents currently held and suppressed; anti-gravity tech; Medbeds capable of curing all disease; alternative energy devices making petroleum and coal redundant;

8. Purified waters of Antarctica will be used to "turn the deserts green" and 'restore mineral life' to all plants and living things.

9. Peace will be established throughout the world as all aggressive activities will cease, and all foreign forces are recalled to their homeland; all current and future nuclear-powered weaponry will be eliminated;

10. Soon, Earth will join "The Galactic Federation of Light" and then live among other off-world races, using the secret space program that has been operating for decades; we will trade with other planets and humanoids and travel to other inhabited worlds;

11. The heart and soul of the US Constitutional laws, for justice, will be the pattern for all courts and legal matters; all judges and attorneys will be re-schooled in these concepts.

Operations were already underway to arrest, try, and deal with members of the Khazarian Mafia worldwide who were behind the corruption, decay, and planned enslavement of all humanity. The military in every GESARA compliant nation led those operations and conducted tribunals for those found to be in league with the evil attempting to destroy humanity and assume ownership and command of all.

Porter understood it was a lot to grasp in a single meeting. So he left the material with each person he talked with privately in their native language. If and when they were prepared to sign on to GESARA, he asked that they contact him.

Porter told each party that inside their folder were two documents explaining the KM — the Khazarian Mafia. "When you read them, you will understand a great deal more about the unseen evil force we have been almost enslaved to."

CHAPTER 17

The present-day Khazarian Mafia (KM) knows it cannot operate or even exist without the cloak of deep secrecy. Therefore, it has spent considerable money and efforts having its history expunged from the history books worldwide. The point was to prevent citizens of the world from learning about this, the largest Organized Crime Cabal in human existence. "Evil beyond imagination" is the label assigned to the organization by those who know of the mafia's existence.

The organized crime organization has the goal of hijacking the whole world with its satanic and pedophilia agenda. It has been exposed as the International Crime Syndicate it is, and its association with Israel has also been revealed. In a 2014 Conference on Combating Terrorism and Religious Extremism, President Putin of Russia was asked to release Russian Intel to expose about 300 traitors in the US Congress. These elected political figures have participated in and personally committed severe serial felonies and statutory espionage — all on behalf of the Khazarian Mafia against America and many Middle East nations. The Khazarian Mafia indeed participated in the 9-11attack on America, as well as the Oklahoma City Murrah Building Bombing in April,1995.

The KM dates back to 100-800 AD. Khazaria was a nation most people have never heard of. The Khazars successfully gained their independence when the Western Turkish Empire broke up after civil wars in the middle of the 7th century. These were Turkic people in Central Asia. The ancient Turkic tribes were quite diverse. Reddish hair was predominant among them before the Mongol conquests. In the beginning, the Khazars believed in Tengri shamanism, which meant "The Eternal Blue Sky." They worship the sky as the principal supporter of their existence in daily prayers. They were nomadic and spoke a Turkic language.

The Khazars were ruled by an evil king, who followed ancient Babylonian black arts and the occult. Their source of income was raiding travelers —individuals and caravans. Khazars become known as thieves, murderers, and road bandits. They assumed the identities of travelers they had murdered. It was an everyday occupational practice and way of life. They were feared and hated by all the people near Khazaria and forced to traverse the Khazar's territory.

The Russians finally applied enough military force to the Khazars to get their attention. With threats of total destruction, the Khazars were told to pick an Arabic theocratic religion and to both teach and live by it. The choices were Islam, Judaism, and Christianity. They chose Judaism — at least publicly. They learned Hebrew and Slavic, and became settlers in cities and towns throughout the North Caucasus and Ukraine. The Khazarians were independent for around 800 years, from the 5th to the 13th century.

They developed into a nation of oligarchs who served as their court. Despite their agreement and promise to the Russian, the Khazarian kings and inner circle kept practicing ancient Babylonian black magic. This Secret Satanism involved occult ceremonies featuring child sacrifice, after "bleeding them out," drinking their blood, and eating their hearts.

The dark secret of these Satanist ceremonies was that they were all based on ancient Baal Worship. The Khazarian kings melded Luciferian black-magic practices with Judaism and created their secret Satanic-hybrid religion. And Khazarians continued their evil ways, robbery, and murder.

In order to stop the Khazarian crimes against their people, the Russians invaded Khazaria along with a group of nations surrounding it 1,200 AD. By this time, the Khazarian king and his inner court had become known as the Khazarian Mafia.

The Khazarian leaders got prior knowledge of the intended invasion. They escaped to Europe. In particular, they went to the nations of western Europe, taking their vast fortune with them in gold and silver with them.

Back in Khazaria, the symbol of their royalty was a shield with a red six-pointed star on it. In their new incarnation, they took the name of "red shield," which translated in German to Rothschild or "child of the rock, Satan." It was under this name they began their fresh rise.

The last Khazarian king and his mafia court swore and plotted eternal revenge against the Russians. Succeeding Khazarian leaders mounted a secret invasion of England. They hired Oliver Cromwell to murder King Charles 1st and set about making England safe for banking. The English Civil Wars raged for nearly a decade and resulted in killing off the true royal family and hundreds of the genuine English nobility. The Khazarians gained control of the City of London. They then set up their banks and made London the banking capital of Europe. This led to the beginning of the British Empire.

The original Rothschild had five sons. As they became adults, their father could infiltrate them into the City of London Central Banking System. Through the use of carrier pigeons, the Rothchilds knew that Napoleon had lost the battle of Waterloo. But they spread the word that the "little corporal" had, in fact, beaten the British. Using this fraud, they were able to buy up British wealth for pennies on the dollar. In turn, they had the money to branch out over Europe as the most powerful bankers in existence. They set up a private Fiat banking system specializing in making counterfeit money from nothing.

Quickly, the Rothschilds hijacked all of England's major institutions — including the British royal family.

In the 1600s, KM fakes were substituted for murdered British Royals. The same process was repeated in the 1700s and French Royals. It was the Khazarians behind the murder of Austrian Archduke

Ferdinand, which kicked off WW1. In 1917, the KM infiltrated and hijacked Russia through their KM army, the Bolsheviks. They murdered the Czar and his family, and stole all the Russian royal's gold, silver, and art treasures. Again, using murder and takeover, the KM murdered the Austrian and German Royals just before WW2. Similarly, they got rid of the Chinese Royals with an infiltrated and hijacked revolutionary army. By the end of WWII, they disempowered the Japanese ruler.

The Rothschilds and the Khazarian Mafia had been behind the world's slave trade before the American Revolution. They, too, controlled the drug trade of all kinds, with Christian nations worldwide being their targets. But nonchristian nations were not exempt. The Boxer Rebellions or the Opium Wars were Chinese wars to escape the drug addictions imposed on them by the KM. To the Rothschilds, the drug trade has always meant tremendous income.

They began the international slave trade in all the New World. Blacks, in particular, became the stock in trade of the Western Hemisphere, while whites were the preferred slaves in the East. The stronger African tribes were paid handsomely to enslave their rivals and neighboring tribes. The whites behind this were susceptible to the diseases of Africa. Thus, blacks became the KM's agents to supply the needed inventory of other blacks.

The Rothschild bankers learned early on that war was their friend. They found they could double their money in short order by lending money to both sides of any warring conflict. They got taxation laws passed to guarantee payment, which could force price. However, when their bankers lost their bets on the American Revolution, they intensified their hatred for Russia. It was the Russians whom they blamed for their losses in the first American conflict. Russia had helped with the blockading of British Ships. They added the United States to their eternal revenge list, along with the Russians. Plotting ways to retake America became a new obsession.

Their attempts to retake America in 1812 failed, again because of Russian interference. The Rothschilds and their KM developed a long-term plan to savage both the US and Russia. They wanted to strip both nations of their natural assets, impose tyranny, and mass-murder their populace.

The KM's first attempt to set up a private American central bank was halted by President Andrew Jackson. Old Hickory called them Satanic and vowed to route them out by the grace and power of Almighty God.

CHAPTER 18

It took until 1913 for Rothschild KM to get their foot in the door of the US. Then, through bribery, crooked and treasonous members of Congress were able to pass the unconstitutional Federal Reserve Act. The bill was passed on Christmas Eve that year — without a required quorum. President Franklin Roosevelt then signed the Act. This ensured that American citizens would pay for government spending without question.

Using their secret fiat counterfeiting of the Federal Reserve, the KM could finance and elect anyone they wanted. Then, relying on their control of a bribed Congress, they created the Internal Revenue Service, which was incorporated in Puerto Rico, and became the KM's private collection agency.

The Rothschild Khazarian Mafia next created the Federal Bureau of Investigation. This new agency was not to fight crime in the US but to protect KM banksters and serve their cover-up needs. Additionally, the FBI began its efforts to curb and prevent, when possible, the prosecution of those taking part in pedophilia networks and child sacrifice rituals. The agency also served as a covert Intel operation for the KM. And yet, the FBI had no right to investigate crimes or pursue anyone.

According to the Library of Congress, it had no official charter until 1979. Before that, it had no right to exist.

The Rothschild KM took over and controlled Judaism, which they falsely embraced hundreds of years before. They passed out wealth and success to those Jews whom they seduced. In time these people began to become witting and unwitting assets. It didn't matter if they were Ashkenazi, Sephardic, and Mizrahi Jews. These different groups differ not so much by racial DNA markers but by heritage.

The KM financed the establishment of the state of Israel. Through the Balfour Declaration of 1917. The decision was made public in a letter from British Foreign Secretary Lord Arthur James Balfour to Lord Walter Rothschild.

The Israeli Knesset, the state's legislative building, was financed and constructed using Freemason occult architecture. The design displayed their commitment to the occult and Babylonian Talmudism — and all the evil accompanying it — including child sacrifice to their secret god Baal. In addition, they created World Zionism, which teaches and instills susceptible Jews with a paranoid group delusion of racial superiority. They promote the idea that all Gentiles were intent on mass-murdering all Jews.

The Rothschilds gained control over the world of banking and the Wall Street professions in general. They likewise control the US Congress and the mass media. Moreover, they exert influence, if not control, through secret societies, the most wealth, and economic means of success — particularly in the West.

During WWII, Hitler became a problem for his KM supporters. Not because of the Holocaust, but by introducing a financial system free of usury and beneficial to the working class. The Rothschilds then mandated the utter destruction of Germany. They could never allow an economic system that did not depend on usury to exist.

The same approach to Islam was the Khazarian war against all Islamic nations. Islam forbids usury. The KM stoked Israel's aggression and instigated the destruction of the Islamic people of the world.

Following WWII, the Rothschild KM developed and pushed the Cold War. It used this time to bring Nazi scientists and mind-control experts to America under Operation Paperclip. This facilitated an expanded worldwide spying and espionage system that far exceeded their prior efforts.

The KM, always playing the long game, continued to infiltrate and subvert all American institutions. This included the various American church systems, Freemasonry (both the Scottish Rite and York Rite), the US military, US Intelligence, and most private defense contractors. They also insinuated themselves into the US Judiciary, both major US political parties, and most agencies of the US government. They slipped unnoticed into the new countries and governments created through the wars supported by the US State Department and CIA worldwide.

With their newly gained private homeland of Israel, their New Khazaria, in 1947, they began triggering their Zionist puppets to acquire all of Palestine. They manipulated dumb American Goyim to fight and die on their behalf. The aim was to take all the Arab lands for Israel so the Khazarians could asset strip their wealth and natural resources, especially their crude oil.

Through bribes and blackmail, critical members of the US Congress and the legislatures in NATO, South and Central America, and the Far East, have inducted vulnerable members into their secret satanic network. The rewards to each were increased status, and power.

The Rothschilds decided to gain complete control over all US and other nations' public education. In the US, for example, they set up the Department of Education. Next, they wrote and wove into schools globalist and socialist curriculums based on political correctness and diversity.

Fluoride was added to the public water and toothpaste. Dentists were mind-controlled through dental schools and manipulated scholarly publications to believe fluoride prevented cavities. The fact was the substance is harmful to both brain and thyroid function.

With vaccinations, programs were developed and deployed to dumb-down children and create vast numbers of future chronic health problems. Moreover, physicians were mind-controlled and misled by biassed research, ignoring any studies countering the KM's goals — even when most scholarly research was usually against any drug, practice, or procedure the KM supported. In addition, all vaccine cell lines are contaminated with a known carcinogenic slow-acting virus, SV-40 (simian virus — which creates rare brain, bone, and lung-related tumors — the exact malignant cancer SV40 causes in lab animals).

The KM used its economic power to control medical schools and set up its controlled American Medical Association. In addition, other medical, dental, and psychological societies were built and/or controlled.

The massive dumbing-down and mind-controlling of the American masses was the KM's plan when buying up and merging all the American mass media. KM agents or operatives purchased six controlled major mass media (CMMM). The CMMM function as an illegal news cartel.

The Rothschild KM Chieftains have now decided it is time to use America to complete their final take-down and occupation of the Whole World. Eleven of the 12 KM leaders call themselves the "Illuminati" or "Disciples of Satan." These men conduct semi-annual child sacrifices in Denver, eat the hearts, and drink children's blood after having sex with them.

The Alliance, nations, and states who will join GESARA and participate in the arrest of the corrupt are the hope of the world. We will all stand together against Rothschild Khazarian Mafia and reclaim a free world's finances, rights, and power. The World's Reset.

CHAPTER 19

After returning to DC following the G-20, Porter's first meeting was with Leon Nickleby, Director of the FBI. The President knew what he was about to do wasn't going to be popular. The picture-perfect, ideal FBI Director was a popular guest on left-wing cable and traditional networks. The 60-year-old broad-shouldered, white blonde-haired, Director could usually present a calm poker face. It was what he had trained himself to do. But he couldn't control himself when Porter told Nickleby he was accepting his letter of resignation. The man's mouth dropped open, and he stood in the Oval Office stunned.

"You're firing me?" Nickleby asked.

"You can spin it any way you'd like to," Porter said. "Our statement is going to be that I accepted your letter of resignation."

"Do you know what information I have on everyone in this town — including you — Mister President?"

"I can only imagine, Leon. But that's the reason I want someone else in your position. Someone I can trust and not someone who is — Deep State."

"This is more trouble than you realize," Nickleby said threateningly.

"Oh, I'm sure. And I also know you will do everything you can to make it so. But this is a Presidential decision. And it's done. You can leave your fed creds and badge here."

Nickleby didn't move a muscle for a moment, then fumbled for his federal credentials and shield. He tossed them past the President to his desk before the now ex-FBI Director turned on his heels and left.

One week after the Senate confirmed Fear of hospital overcrowding, massive corpse piles, PPE for health workers, both the nominated Secretary of the Interior and another public confirmation hearing were slated. The second confirmation hearing was for Porter's nominee to be the new Director of the FBI.

It had taken Porter a week's worth of jawboning to get 48-year-old Texas Ranger Captain Konner Ochoa to accept the nomination.

Konner was of average height and weight. He had an oval face, quick light coffee brown eyes almost the same color as his skin. His light-colored Western hat sat on the table before him. He wore a white shirt and a tie which matched his suit — a tan Western cut jacket and trousers, and polished brown cowboy boots. His tie pin was a miniature Texas Ranger badge.

Senator Hartman Vanderpool, Republican, was a member of the nomination committee. The 73-year-old Georgian was more of an Independent than a strict Republican. Vanderpool sported flaring red and gray eyebrows on his long face.

"Captain Ochoa," the Senator began his question, "do you like musicals?"

Vanderpool liked to throw witnesses off their planned game and scripted answers.

It took a moment for the Ranger to wrinkle his forehead and think. Ella Suzuki and Ward Adair had told him to be quick, honest, and straightforward, with his responses to all questions. "Some," he said.

"My wife likes them more than I do — but there are a couple I don't mind — like The Music Man, Flower Drum Song, and...."

"The Music Man," the Senator cut Konner off. That's one of my favorites, too. But you know, I never can figure out how everyone — like in the library scene — you know, the "Madam Liberian" scene?"

"Yes, Senator."

"Now how in blue blazes do all the folks in there automatically know all the dance steps? And the words to the song?"

"It's not realistic," Konner said.

"Absolutely. Now, the reason I bring this up is because of what one of the traveling salesmen keeps saying in the very first scene — remember, the one on the train?"

The Texas Ranger Captain nodded his head.

"This salesman keeps saying, 'But you've got to know the territory.' That's my question to you, Captain Ochoa. You've never been an FBI agent. Do you think you know the territory?"

"I know law enforcement -- policing, on the beat, on patrol, investigations, and I know law enforcement administration."

"From the Texas Rangers — but not the FBI."

"Senator, we all know the reputation of the FBI has been seriously tarnished in the last few years. Like Harold Hill in The Music Man, I may not know this territory, but I think I know the FBI's got trouble — big trouble — that starts with 't' and rhymes with "p," and that stands for police. The President told me he was looking for someone not from inside the FBI but from the outside. Someone who could see the organization from a different perspective. I think I have that perspective."

"Are you saying, 'A new broom sweeps clean?'" Senator Vanderpool asked.

"Could be," Konner said. "Sometimes a good cleaning is needed — but sometimes all that's needed is a straightening up — washing the windows to let more light in."

"Transparency."

"Yes, sir."

"What if it takes more than that?"

"I've washed many a dish, Senator, swept and mopped many a floor. And I know how to take out the trash."

"Then you've got my vote, Captain. And I encourage my colleagues to do the same."

CHAPTER 20

The COVID situation had worsened since Porter had attended the G-20. He met with the Vice President and the CDC team on the couches in the Oval Office. Dr. Sinead Trench, whom some in the media had labeled "the broach lady." The adornment she wore this day was not one Porter had seen before. -- and it was striking, as usual. He secretly wondered if she collected broaches like some women collected shoes.

The Director of the National Institute of Allergies and Infectious Diseases spoke on behalf of the trio of health professionals.

"There are confirmed infections in 43 states," she reported. "We will be asking all governors to set up testing stations — throughout the states, not just in the cities. Thanks to Vice President Holyoak, we have a distribution arrangement for testing kits to be shipped nationwide on an emergency basis."

"Do we know any more about where this disease came from?" Porter wanted to know. "China, but where — specifically. Wuhan — but where there?"

"We suspect," Dr. Trench said, "an open food market. It's a place that deals in all types of animals and plants. With the help of the

Chinese, we are trying to narrow down a more exact site. Even patient zero if we can find him or her."

Porter looked over to Tracy Holyoak.

"The Task Force is up and running. But, until we know more, all we can do is address the needs of front-line workers — in hospitals, EMTs, police, and firefighters."

"Why don't you take the lead in the news conference this afternoon — and going forward — until we know what we're doing. Then, Doctors, you should all go to our daily press briefings and be ready to address any questions which are medical in nature."

"Yes, Sir," everyone in the room agreed.

"I've already talked preliminarily with Howard and Saundra," the VP said. "Saundra has official notices about the new director of the FBI and the new Secretary of Interior. The printed copies of those will likely cover our bases there. But, of course, Howard will still helm the podium and be ready to answer any question beyond the immediate medical concerns — although we don't expect there to be many."

"Anything we should anticipate?" Porter asked.

"We may need a nationwide shutdown and hold in place order — at some point — soon," Dr. Trench said. "No spreader events — concerts, plays, festivals, sporting events, cruise ships — it might even come down to recommending no family gatherings — even for holiday celebrations — or birthdays."

"That could be a recommendation — but I don't have the power to order such a thing."

"Even in the event of a national medical emergency?" Dr. Trench acted as if Porter wasn't getting the severity of the situation.

"Even then. The Constitution is clear on that," he looked over at Graham Newcome, his Chief-of-Staff, "isn't it, Graham?"

"I believe you're right, Sir. 'The powers not delegated to the United States by the Constitution, nor prohibited by it to the states, are reserved to the States respectively, or to the people.' Tenth amendment. There is no law that I'm aware of that would allow this office to mandate such a thing."

"We can talk to the governors," Porter said. "They would have such authority — if they chose to use it."

"Well, whatever it takes, Mr. President," Dr. Trench said, sitting back as if having been rebuked.

In the press briefing that followed their meeting in the Oval Office with the President, Drs. Judson Whitehead (Beeker) and Laurennie Jarry, were never called on. However, Dr. Sinead Trench maintained attention once she was asked the first question.

A half-hour into the briefing Demona Enock, 30s, strawberry blonde WOLF Cable Network's White House reporter, asked a key question. "Wearing face masks is normal in Japan. Is this virus something we can protect ourselves against by wearing surgical face masks?"

"No," Dr. Trench answered casually. "Face masks won't have any effect."

Portly liberal TV cable news reporter Abner Moss asked, "Will the CDC be giving us updates? And if so, how often?"

"As Vice President Holyoak said, her COVID Task Force will be meeting daily and will report whatever they have — when appropriate. From the medical side, we at the CDC will do the same. So I think you can expect to see me here every day for some time to come."

Another media reporter, Steve Odili, late 30s, a clean-shaven white South African with a full head of curly dark hair, asked, "What you are telling us is that this disease is going to affect the entire world."

"I said most of it," Dr. Trench interrupted the reporter before he could pose his question. "There will be isolated pockets of population with little or no contact with the larger world whom we expect to have zero to minuscule effects. From what we can tell at this moment, the pathogen is transmitted human to human, although we are not sure how. If some people have contact with only uninfected individuals, they will probably be unaffected."

"My question," the reporter picked up, "is — can we expect the United States to take the lead in controlling, treating, and even preventing this disease?"

"We have the best scientists and physicians in the world working on this at the CDC. I am certain other nations will do the same with their agencies similar to ours. Like China, for example. The CDC hopes we find treatment methods of controlling the spread — but at this time, no one knows a great deal about it. Our scientists and physicians are trying to unravel the genome of COVID and will announce our findings as quickly as possible. We are also working in conjunction with the World Health Organization. We will examine any protocols they may offer, and we will turn our findings over to the entire world."

The Associated Press's Miranda Bank, 53, cornflower blue eyes seen through her horn-rimmed glasses, kept a spare ballpoint pen in the tight bun of her blond and gray hair. Her question was, "How fast should we expect this pathogen to spread — and to what percentage of those who contract the disease will it be fatal?"

"Neither of those statistics we've been able to pin down. I'll provide the numbers to you as soon as we know them. Unfortunately, we are guessing there will be significant casualties — but among exactly what populations we simply do not know yet. We are not optimistic for anyone with severe immune deficiencies. How this will manifest itself and precisely who among the already compromised will be the most affected are still unknowns.

"Our first suggestion is that people get tested. We are setting up nationwide testing. It's called PCR testing and we are going to provide this to everyone — administered by medical professionals.

"Next, the public should begin using over-the-counter hand sanitizers. We don't know this will help, but we are positive it will do no harm as a precaution.

"The true state of our knowledge about COVID," Dr. Trench seemed to wrap up her answering questions for this day, "is more of an unknown than a body of knowledge at this point. As we gain insights and understandings, I will offer them to you daily."

CHAPTER 21

Porter oversaw the swearing-in of Secretary of the Interior Linton Ston and he began to think such events were one of his prime duties. He had done the same for all the heads of the 15 executive departments.

The next such duty he took part in was that of his new FBI director, Konner Ochoa. This time, the ceremony took place in the East Room. Konner's wife, Alyssa, and two teenage sons were in attendance, along with the entire White House media corps.

Porter's remarks were brief, but he mentioned how he had met the former Texas Ranger after he had been shot in the arm.

"My charge to you, Mr. Director," Porter said, "is to make us proud of the FBI again — whatever that takes. In your confirmation hearing, you said you knew how to take out the trash. If that's what it requires, you have my full support. There are too many front-line FBI agents, criminologists, and others who have been doing their duties faithfully. It seems to me that the problems come largely from FBI headquarters here in Washington, DC. You are the new Director of the FBI, Konner Ochoa. You are not *my FBI Director* but the Director of the FBI for the people. Congratulations."

Kommer stepped up to the podium, holding his white Resistol hat in his hands.

"Thank you, Mr. President. One of the hardest parts of assuming the position will be not wearing my hat every day, everywhere."

This line drew laughter from the crowd.

"But it will be, I'm sure, one of the last things on my mind. Over my career as a Texas Department of Public Safety officer and then as a Texas Ranger, I have worked with many FBI agents. Many I consider more than colleagues but friends. Their work ethics, their professional attitude, and behavior are what I hope to instill in this organization. Once it was every member of the FBI's code. It will be again."

Konner stepped back as those in attendance applauded, including Porter. His thought was that now he had a full cabinet appointed, confirmed, and on the job.

At the exact moment of Konner Ochoa's swearing-in, his predecessor, 60-year-old Leon Nickleby, arrived at the lair of cabal head, Jerren Glowicki. The multi-billionaire used his lodge near Panther Mountain in the New York Adirondacks as his Eagle's Nest.

The broad-shouldered, white blonde-haired former FBI Director was shown into the dark but indirectly lighted office of the key figure behind the New World Order.

The two men didn't shake hands as Nickleby was aware of Glowicki's rare genetic skin condition, *ichthyosis*, which produced red, scaly skin.

"Are you sure you're not being tracked?" Glowicki asked before anything else.

"I left my cell phone at home, and I personally scanned by clothes and my car. Remember, I know all the tricks of the trade — and I'm clean. I even made sure by changing cars twice."

"I expected nothing less," the 79-year-old conspirator said. "Do you know why you were replaced? Who compromised you?"

"I don't believe I was compromised. I think Randall is cleaning his house and wanted his friend, the cowboy, in my office."

"For the moment, I'll accept your word for it."

"What can I do to help the cause?" Nickleby asked.

"Go take a vacation. A very public vacation. Somewhere where you can't be extradited. Brazil is lovely, I understand, this time of year. Take your time and establish yourself there — as someone who wants to be left alone. Then, work out a plan to slip away. I'll send you a burner phone with a contact number on it. Don't use it for anything else."

"Understood."

"For the moment, we need to see how much 'house cleaning' your replacement does. Then we'll know what our next move should be there."

"Should I get a boyfriend down there — to make it look as if I just don't care who knows I'm gay anymore?"

"No. Any companion could cause us trouble when you slip away. It will be better not to leave a body for the police to investigate. Keep your sexual partners to one-night stands. Use some known male prostitutes, if you must. But never anyone more than a single time."

"Whatever you say."

"You were important in your FBI position, but you are still instrumental, Leon. The important thing is for you to remain available. COVID is our key operation. So, stay healthy, and don't let anyone give you a shot of any kind."

"Yes, sir."

Leon Nickleby turned and left.

Secretary of Defense Victor Chesterfield and the select members of the Joint Chiefs-of-Staff stood as the President entered the PEOC for their regular meeting. The military officers all saluted, and Porter returned their salutes. Then they all sat, except for the Defense remained standing.

"Mr. President, we have been able to clear Vice President Holyoak and her husband, your Chief-of-Staff, Mr. Graham Newcome, your personal secretary, Ms. Gwendolyn Jacobs, as well as your communications team — Ms. Saundra Fontana and Mr. Howard X. Sterling. Each have seen some of the material we provided you, Sir, and the First Lady — but not all — enough for them to know the outline of the Cabal threat."

"Thank you," Porter said. "That makes my life a little easier. I don't have to be on guard at all times."

"We are also working on your new White House photographer —," the Secretary of Defense glanced at his notes, "— Mr. Harris Ozman and some strategic members of your cabinet — names are on this list. We've already cleared your FBI Director."

Porter nodded his head. "It will be good to know who all I can speak to about this."

"It won't be everyone, Mr. President. This is still a sensitive operation."

"Oh, I've got that."

"I would also like to tell you that your security briefing team is good. Ms. Grace Spurlock and Rear Admiral Matthew Stott, the new Director of the NSA, have been vetted. So has Lt. Colonel Bruce Ellison and his partner, Lt. Col. Alan Coughlin, who are in charge of the 'football.' They can be trusted. However, not all of your Secret Service bodyguards are clear. The pair who came from Texas with you, Agents Melissa McBride and Joe Lamb, are OK."

"You have been doing a lot of clearing," Porter said.

"We're trying to help you, Mr. President. This is still the most highly secret operation we have. We've not read in anyone in Congress, nor any member of the Supreme Court. It's very much 'need-to-know.' And some of those I've named for you tonight are not privy to much of it — but they know that everything about Operation Odin is to be guarded."

Victor handed Porter a single page of cleared names.

CHAPTER 22

Michael Robertson had become almost a saint to the BLM and ANTIFA movements. Professionally created and produced posters with Robertson's picture, encircled with flowers or framed as if in a Catholic church alcove, became common in ongoing "peaceful protests." Unfortunately, such protests invariably turned into mob violence across the nation — violence that progressive and liberal media attempted to justify.

Yancy Day-French, Howard Sterling's on-air replacement at INK, was one defender of the protesters. The early 30s, California pretty boy with symmetrical features and carefully coffered hair, often slipped into an editorial mode on his evening newscast.

"Whoever said protesters had to be peaceful. Of course, there will be damage and destruction of property. These people are upset, angry, and feel unheard. They are lashing out in the only ways they know-how. They have a right to be angry."

One protester told a WOLF live broadcast that he came from New Mexico but was frustrated in Houston. Wearing a blue bandana across his face, the oily-haired young man said he had yet to see any of the $15 an hour he had signed up for. He had been provided food and transportation — on a bus full of other protesters — but he was tiring of protesting and not getting paid.

When four Little Rock police officers were shot and killed during one protest, Porter called in Department of Homeland Security Chief Winford Mead. The stocky, 56-year-old, retired full bird colonel from the Military Police still kept his gray hair -- buzz cut with white sidewalls. He had keen dark eyes and a propionate Adam's apple. Mead sat on a couch opposite the President in the Oval Office.

"It's all politics," Mr. President. "Either the mayor and/or the governor is a democrat -- or they are afraid of offending their black constituency."

"I've already gone over posse comitatus with Victor Chesterfield."

"I've discussed it with him, too, Sir. But if the local authorities don't get a handle on this, you still have a duty to protect the American citizens. Some polls suggest your doing something has the approval of at least forty percent of the population."

"Polls I don't care about, Winford. Being legal, however, is important to me. But, at the same time, I will not allow this to continue while we just sit and watch."

"I'm with you, Mr. President." The DHS Secretary sat forward, his forearms on his knees. "I've made some unofficial calls to the National Guard Commanders in Oregon, California, Indiana, Illinois, and Arkansas. But, unfortunately, there's not a consensus among them. They all say they could put these riots down in one night — but they worry about the political implications of doing so. A couple of them say they won't do anything without specific, written orders from their governors or from you."

The President sat back on his couch. Then, when he spoke, he sat back up.

"How about the money behind these riots? The pre-positioned bricks — printed signs — and paid protesters?"

"That money is hard to track. We have confirmed that those who are paid are always paid in cash."

"What about BLM and ANTIFA?"

"They're the driving forces," the former military police officer said. "And both have GoFundMe pages and their websites, which will accept donations. They're funded with big corporate money, beyond individual donations. I'm talking a million or two before any of this current eruption. It's my belief they have been just waiting for a reason to riot."

"But our hands are tied," President Randall said, tightening his jaw, "— at least for the moment."

"Yes, Sir. I'm afraid so."

The spring Rose Garden wedding of Grant Yarbrough to Therese Herzog was a unique event. The 34-year-old former CNN News anchor, son of a Vietnamese mother and a black U.S. Air Force sergeant, had been White House Press Secretary under former President Leo Gibson. Grant had continued in that position when Porter suddenly became President.

The bride, now 37, was a Communications Ph.D. from Wisconsin, and was also a holdover from the Gibson administration. Theresa continued as a speechwriter under Porter. Her best physical feature was her genuine smile. She wore round glasses, which did little to flatter her pale gray eyes and round face. This day, her curly chestnut hair was penned up under her white veil.

The President had the honor of walking the bride down the aisle. However, those attending the wedding were seated six feet apart, as per the latest CDC health guidelines. As a result, elbow bumps instead of handshakes were the order of the day.

Still, there was much hugging the bride and kisses on her cheeks.

For a honeymoon, the pair was traveling fiords and sites of Norway, Sweden, and Denmark. Then they were off to Puerto Rico, the bride's home. This was also where the couple had worked together to restore full electrical power repair roads, bridges, and rooftops. Therese was now ready to begin her campaign to become the territory's first female governor. Grant was to be her campaign manager and then her Attorney General.

New White House photographer Harris Ozman was a multi-Pulitzer Prize winner. He covered the event both for the White House but also for the couple. He had begun his career as a wedding photographer and found he enjoyed capturing posed and casual moments of the event.

Ozman was boney, with a sparse van dyke beard and mustache. At 41, his wide-set pewter eyes had a sense of proportion and framing. The resulting shot from his Nikon D750 DSLR with 24 to 120mm zoom were colorful, arresting, and simply beautiful images. He had pictures that proved the wedding guests were spaced correctly, but the bride and groom were hardly separated from the moment of their spoken vows.

To the outside world, the CDC guidelines' observance was more clearly an exercise in violations. Regardless of the lovely and touching moments of the event, the hugs and kisses were denounced mainly by the media. This was expected, especially because the media was barred from the occasion at the couple's request.

"What were they hiding?" was the liberal cry from the progressive press and cable news outlets before the wedding. Afterward, they used Harris Ozman's pictures to prove that the White House gave only lip service to COVID. Instead, the majority of the media sometimes issued hysterical warnings. The left claims that the spreading and growing infections were the new Black Death.

CHAPTER 23

Dr. Sinead Trench, Director of the National Institute of Allergies and Infectious Diseases, spoke to the now space-separated reporters in the White House Briefing Room.

"The reason you are separated is because of the CDC's latest recommendations for fighting COVID. They are:"

1. Stay at a distance of at least 6 feet from other people;

2. Wash hands regularly with soap and water. If that's not possible, use hand sanitizer or disinfecting wipes;

3. Avoid touching your face; and

4. Monitor daily for symptoms such as fever, cough, and shortness of breath."

The points appeared on the TV monitors on either side of Dr. Trench as she read them out.

"Call your health care provider or local hospital," she continued, "if symptoms develop to see if you should be tested for COVID. You all have been provided with a printed copy of these guidelines.

"The exploding COVID infections have led us (meaning the CDC) to fear hospital overcrowding, a shortage of personal protective equipment — PPE — for health workers. We've been able to identify the most vulnerable population — the elderly. Particularly the elderly with current infectious diseases and other underlying chronic medical conditions — such as obesity, heart, and lung problems.

"There is a need for ventilators. There was a national stockpile of these, but that reserve has been seriously depleted for some reason. So president Randall has put out a call for manufacturers to replenish this urgent need."

Doy Urbie, the Associated Press White House correspondent, asked the first question. "These ventilators — what do they do for a patient?"

"They breathe for a patient whose lungs are too infected or exhausted to do so themselves."

"If there was a national stockpile," the reporter followed up with, "what happened to it?" Urbie, of middle-eastern extraction, had dark sand-colored skin and close-cropped hair, was respected by other White House press corps members. He was known to be fair, but assertive. "I don't recall any demand for ventilators before this."

"Why the stockpile is almost depleted, I cannot say," Dr. Trench answered. "All I am sure of is the urgent demand we now have and that the administration is working on the issue."

"Without these ventilators," Buzz Yeager, INK's middle-aged correspondent, asked, "what do you expect?" Yeager wore his tortoise-shell bifocals parked on his thinning brown hair as he continued his question. "Since you seem to imply that they are so vital."

"They are indeed vital. However, what we expect from the shortage is — massive fatalities."

"How massive?" Demona Enock, the 30s, strawberry blonde WOLF cable network's reporter, asked.

"It is difficult to give you numbers — but I wouldn't be surprised to see more bodies than funeral homes can handle. We might see refrigerated semi-trailers deployed to handle the number of bodies."

Ms. Enock asked, "How about masks for the public? If this is a respiratory infection, can it be spread and contracted by our breath?"

"Yes," Dr. Trench answered and then sighed before she explained. "A few weeks ago, we were concerned about having sufficient masks for hospitals and front-line workers. But we've determined that physicians need M-95 masks — due to their close contact with already infected patients. For the public, paper masks will work very well. You should be able to find them and hand sanitizer at any local drugstore."

The Vice President told the President, "Several members of my Task Force are reaching out to makers and medical equipment companies. What we are trying to do is to see if manufacturers of washing machines and other small appliances, commercial airplane parts, and even military contractors can help."

"They'll need parts, to begin with," Porter said.

"Yes, Sir. All of these people will understand that. Some will take on the job of creating the parts. Others will be able to do the assembly work once converted from their primary function.

"I have to say, Mr. President," Tracy said, "it warms my heart to see how quickly companies, large and small, are stepping up."

"Oh, I forgot to mention," the VP said, "there are several small and local craft brewers who have already started changing over so they can produce hand sanitizer.

"That's the America I know," President Randall smiled. "Why are we not up to the strategic levels we should be?"

"The Strategic Stockpile of medical items, Mr. President," said Saundra Fontana, Director of Whitehouse Communications, "have been largely ignored by the past two administrations according to what I've learned." The middle-aged blonde with hints of gray stood with the Vice President, and Porter's Chief-of-Staff, Graham Newcome, stood in the President's study. Porter had his tie loosened, and his sleeves rolled up.

"Graham," Porter said, "I want this fixed."

The rail-thin, pockmarked-faced Chief-of-Staff had his smartphone in his hands, and he was messaging someone. "I'm on it," he said without looking up.

"There are estimates from the New York Times and on INK cable," Saundra said, "— for what they are worth — that the US will need roughly one million ventilators. That's more than five times what we have on hand.

"Ventilators are expensive and complex machines," VP Tracy Holyoak said. "They can't be churned out in the thousands overnight."

Saundra spoke again, "New York Governor Clark Koke says his state desperately needed 30,000 ventilators, maybe 40,000. He said they only have 12,000. Koke claims they will run out of ventilators in six days at the current burn rate."

"The squeaky wheel gets the grease," Porter said. "Tracy, see what we can do for Koke. He's holding daily news conferences, so let's get him what we can."

"Yes, Sir," she said.

Graham looked up from this phone and explained, "The Strategic National Stockpile (SNS) stockpiles essentially come in three types — medical, defense, and commodities. In addition, each service branch keeps its own pre-positioned stocks of war materiel. These include petroleum and 'rare earth' elements." He glanced down at his phone and continued. "As far as civilians are concerned, our stockpile is managed by the Office of the Assistant Secretary for Preparedness and Response (ASPR). The Director reports to both the Department of Homeland Security and the Department of Health and Human Services. The Office of the Assistant Secretary for Preparedness and Response (ASPR) now handles it under HHS. They have stockpiles of medications and supplies for both military and civilian personnel. FEMA gets its supplies from this stockpile."

"Good to know, Graham," Porter said. He turned to the Vice President. "Tracy, if we need to tap the military stockpile, let's do so on a limited basis."

"Yes, Sir. We will get geared up to replenish and respond to all the needs ASAP. It's the Task Force's prime focus at the moment. But we're also trying to ensure the corner drugstore and supermarkets have face masks, hand sanitizer, and surgical gloves for good measure. And —," the VP paused, "— there are also shortages of certain drugs and medications."

"That should be easy to fix, shouldn't it?" Porter asked.

"You'd think so, Mr. President, but most of our drugs are made in foreign countries."

"How did that happen?" Porter wanted to know.

"I think its part of the 'build a better China' agenda of the Gibson and Obama administrations," Graham said sarcastically.

"Then this is just the kick in the pants to bring those drug-making jobs back home. Graham, get hold of Inez Ceely. And set up a meeting tomorrow with her and both Ward and Ella."

Graham made himself a note on his phone, "Yes, Sir." Inez Ceely was the White House Congressional Liaison. Both Ward Adair and Ella Suzuki had highly recommended her.

"How about hospital space?" the President asked, turning back to the Vice President. "Can we send a hospital ship to New York and some others to places that might be needed?"

"I'll speak to the Defense Secretary about that. And I know a couple of non-prophets who might help with emergency hospitals. They have done so in the past. Even quicker than FEMA."

"Great idea," Porter smiled.

"We may want to make use of some military personal to supplement doctors, nurses, and other hospital staff," Saundra offered.

"That's good, too," the President said. Then to everyone, he said, "Let's all try to get ahead of this, so we don't have to play catch up."

CHAPTER 24

Porter's next secured video conference with his COVID advisors began on a Thursday morning. The monitor on the President's desk was split into four images, one of them being his. Dr. Angelyn Cisneros, a teaching and research faculty member at Florida State University's College of Medicine, spoke first.

"Mr. President," the Hispanic physician with double dimpled cheeks and a gap between her two upper front teeth said, "I think there may be a correlation between the media reports of COVID and the number of cases reported. The elderly, those with co-morbidity, are the most affected, without a doubt. And these cases are genuine — but I've noted a significant drop in this year's annual flu. The samples the World Health Organization has failed to provide have led us to examine virus cells from our patients. What we've found isn't that different from what we expect of a mutation of the flu."

"Are you saying, Doctor," Porter asked, "that there might not be a distinct COVID infection after all?"

"I'm not ready to make that kind of pronouncement," said the woman with full lips and dark hair.

Doctor Cyril Haines, 50, a Ph.D. and an MD, black with a broad nose and small ears, was a professor in the Department of Pathology at

Duke University in Durham, North Carolina. "But this virus is novel because it started with an animal population -- according to the WHO — and it was transmitted to a human somehow. But now, it can go from human to human. And we're seeing the same things Dr. Cisneros is. Still, our immune systems have never seen this particular strain of virus before — even if it is a mutation for last year's flu. Humans simply haven't developed an immunity to it."

Dr. Ravi Khan, MD, Ph.D., and JD, with Dartmouth College's Geisel School of Medicine, was the department chair of the Microbiology and Immunology Department. He had tawny skin, a thick dark mustache, and a bald head.

His contribution was about the symptoms of COVID.

He said, "There is something curious about the difference between the symptoms of COVID and the seasonal flu. COVID presents with fever, cough, shortness of breath, and muscle aches. The flu has all of the above, plus headaches and a runny nose. Why the difference?

"We too have seen the similarities, Dr. Cisneros and Dr. Haines noted. And we are examining the molecules from our patients. But is what we're seeing COVID or a new flu? Unfortunately, I can't get an example from the CDC or the WHO, either."

"What are each of you using as a treatment regiment?" Porter asked.

Dr. Cisneros said, "Recommendation that people stay home and isolate themselves until they become cyanotic, turning blue from lack of oxygen, is a disgrace. What are the people at the CDC doing? We are now waiting for the virus to trigger the cytokine storm in some people. And when they arrive in that state, it's challenging to reverse it and stop it and bring them back."

From Duke University, Doctor Haines said, "We know how to treat inflammation and blood clotting with corticosteroids and anticoagulants. Unfortunately, press releases from the CDC failed to include any information from clinicians treating COVID patients. There seems to be little interest in spelling out what the specific COVID symptoms are or in detailing what physicians and hospitals need to do."

From Dartmouth, Dr. Khan said, "We — and from some reports --

doctors around the world — are using the anti-malaria drug hydroxychloroquine (HCQ). It's an off-label use, but it works."

"With our elderly patients," Dr. Haines said, "we have found that HCQ suppresses the patient's natural built-up antiviral defenses. Together with azithromycin and zinc sulfate, we've had a 100% success rate for just five days. No, we did lose one patient, but she had several co-morbidities we could not treat. But for all the rest — they walked out of here on their own feet."

"Thank you for saying that, Drs," Dr. Cisneros said from Florida. "We've discovered the same thing — particularly with our elderly patients. But when I reported this to the CDC, they didn't seem interested. So don't they understand this virus — or do they, for some reason, not want to treat it?"

"So, it's the cytokine storm," Porter said, "that actually kills people. The shutting down of their organs in mass."

"Yes, in the elderly." Dr. Kahn said. "They have such a strong immune system which always tries to fight the virus — but the virus replicates faster than their natural defenses can respond."

"And," Dr. Haines added, "HCQ stops the replication of the virus."

"But it's not a cure-all," Dr. Kahn said. "This is working for older people. Middle-aged and younger — we don't want to suppress the immune system — but it still halts the virus."

"Why doesn't the CDC know this?" Porter asked partly to himself, "and why aren't they asking those who know?"

"You, Mr. President," Dr. Cisneros said, "are the one to ask that question."

"Yes, I am," Porter said. "And I intend to."

CHAPTER 25

Before the next day's presser, President Randall sat on a couch across from Dr. Sinead Trench. The two were alone in the Oval Office.

"How long has it been since you've treated patients, Dr. Trench?" Then, the President cut right to the critical aspect.

"Mr. President, I am primarily a researcher — and administrator."

"I understand and respect that, Dr. But it doesn't answer my question," Porter said. "Personally treating patients — how long ago?"

Dr. Trench fingered her Blue Morpho butterfly broach on the left chest of her yellow pants suit. She was uncomfortable with the direction this conversation was going.

"I treated patients —" she paused and didn't seem to want to go on.

"As an intern — according to the information I have." Porter notices Dr. Trench lick her lips, which, although colored, seemed suddenly dry.

"A researcher's focus is not so much on treating the individual, Sir. It's more about investigating and discovering new and innovative cures."

"And approving drugs from Big Pharma," the President pressed.

Porter saw the color drain from the face of the 63-year-old Director of the National Institute of Allergies and Infectious Diseases at the Center for Disease Control and Prevention.

"Older — cheaper drugs seem to have little of your focus or interest. Or am I wrong?"

"I'm not sure want you're getting at, Mr. President."

"Then I'll spell it out, Dr. Anti-malaria hydroxychloroquine — HCQ. You know it. And I believe you know that along with a regimen of azithromycin and zinc sulfate will heal an elderly COVID patient who otherwise is in relatively good to excellent health — in a few days. Am I correct?"

"Well, there have been some — very scattered reports —."

"From clinically patient treating physicians around the world," Porter finished the thought the CDC representative didn't seem to want to.

"These are anecdotal reports. Not statistical backed studies," the nervous Dr. Trench said. She realized she was fingering her broach and dropped her hand back to her lap.

"And these treatments of existing medicines are pennies on the dollar to what any cure you, your colleagues, or any of the major drug companies might come up with. Are there any such studies underway to prove or disprove these reports?"

"Well — no. We have been looking forward to more inclusive — newer treatments."

"Do you have any reason to disbelieve the positive reports you've received?"

It took the physician/administrator a moment to try and come up with a more sophisticated answer, but finally had to settle for a simple, "No, Sir, we don't."

"So is the CDC, and specifically your agency, merely ignorant — or is there a financial motive from the outside which is pushing your lack of medical curiosity?"

Dr. Trench swallowed before she spoke. When she did, she said, "No, Sir. I will see that funds and personnel are assigned to such a study the moment I return to my office."

"Excellent, Dr.," Porter said. "And another thing you will do is you will not in any way discount or diminish what I am going to say in the

Press Briefing before you say a word. If you do, you will consider yourself fired when you exit the Press Room. Am I clear?"

"Yes, Sir," she said softly — her eyes on her matching yellow shoes.

The separated and mask-wearing media reporters got to their feet when Porter entered the Press Room and stepped up on the platform.

"Please be seated," he said.

Porter took a moment before he spoke. "I have something to report to you. It's not a discovery of any breakthrough new drug but a treatment regimen using existing medicines. And this is not for everyone. It is primarily for the elderly — those in good to excellent health but who have been infected with COVID."

The reporters were making notes and were totally engaged in the President's remarks.

"What I'm talking about is the off-label use of a drug originally developed for malaria. Off-label means prescribing a drug to treat a condition for which the Food and Drug Administration has not approved. It's called hydroxychloroquine — HCQ." The word was spelled out on the TV monitors behind the President. "Some physicians from around the world have developed the treatment for this drug along with azithromycin — you may know it as Zmax. It is an antibiotic. It's used to treat several bacterial infections. To name a few — middle ear infections, strep throat, pneumonia, traveler's diarrhea, and certain other intestinal infections. Zinc sulfate is an inorganic compound most often used as a dietary supplement to treat zinc deficiency and prevent the condition in those at high risk. It is also be used to treat malaria. A combination of these readily available relatively inexpensive drugs — taken in the correct five-day regimen — will cure an elderly patient who is otherwise in good health."

"Cure?" The word was repeated throughout the room by the reporters.

"That's what treating physicians have found. So the CDC, as I'm sure Dr. Trench will verify in a few moments, will start a study to prove the efficacy of this treatment. And I want to point out this is primarily for elderly patients. But then, those are the most likely to be hit with COVID from what we know so far."

"I'll take a few questions and then turn this over to Dr. Trench." Porter pointed to Irish Leftwich, the 4 foot 1 inch, full-figured MSNBC White House reporter on the front row.

"I'm Irish Leftwich — MSNBC —You aren't wearing a mask, Mr. President."

"Is that a question?"

"Yes, sir," the nut brown-eyed journalist with butch short hair said.

"Well, I'm neither about to perform surgery nor attempting to rob a convenience store. So, no, I am not wearing a mask."

"But the CDC guidelines suggest we do."

"Simply because a government agency suggests something doesn't mean it's an order which everyone must obey on penalty of fines, jail time, or death. I am a former surgeon — as you may remember. I've seen the CDC recommendations. I've also spent time masked while operating. To mask or not to mask is a decision each individual must make. I have chosen not to. And before you ask and we go down this rabbit hole, I've not asked that anyone in the White House wear a mask. They are free to do so if they like. The paper and cloth masks available in the drug store and on supermarket shelves aren't of much value. Have you ever been on an elevator and suddenly smelled the evidence that it was Taco Tuesday?"

The reporters laughed. Many did so despite themselves.

"We could put them on cows, but I doubt it would satisfy those who believe it is bovine flatulence that is a major factor in the warming of our climate. The only masks that are effective are the M-95s. Now, do I have any questions about hydroxychloroquine?" Porter pointed to Doy Urbie.

The forty-something reporter stood and said, "Doy Urbie, the Associated Press. Because you are an MD, Mr. President, even if you are not a practicing physician, some people will take this as medical advice."

"I'm sure you're right. So, I will say, this is not a prescription, and what I am saying here about hydroxychloroquine — or masks — is NOT to be considered a prescription. Instead, I am offering you some medical *information* about HCQ. And my decision about masks is my own. Therefore, ambulance chasers need not call or write."

This line produced a chuckle from the Press Room.

"What I would advise is for each individual to check with their personal physician and even get a second opinion if they feel they need to. All physicians don't agree on everything. And they shouldn't. There are conflicting studies — and every human reacts in their own unique way to anything introduced into their body — infections and treatments. I encourage people to act with care — whatever that means for them. For some, it will mean wearing a mask when they are by themselves — alone in their car or even at home. However, let's not become a nation of shamers and bigots. Other people will not feel the need to mask — anywhere — anytime. We still have freedom of choice in this country. So, to each their own. Follow what advice you feel is true for you. Even do your own research. The Internet is full of facts — and falsehoods. Decide what is right for you."

"Then, if I may, Mr. President, I'd like to ask about the advisability of using any medication for a purpose for which it was not created."

"In the late '80s, Pfizer was looking for a treatment for heart-related chest pain. But in their clinical trials, they were disappointed with their findings. However, other things kept coming up. Now, this was a drug they hoped would sell millions of pills. Then, in the trials, it looked like it was a bust. Then they looked at one of the side effects and marketed the new drug for an off-label use. You may have heard of it — some of you may have even used it. It's called Viagra."

The Press Room exploded with laughter.

When it died down, the President said, "What I'm saying is sometimes an off-label use can be a delightful surprise."

CHAPTER 26

INK, CNN, and MSMBC all reported that the President had recommended Viagra as a COVID cure. Likewise, the late-night talk shows all had jokes about the idea.

The President wasn't surprised to receive a visit from HHS Secretary Talmage Goughenbaugh the next morning. The squat fifty-eight-year-old with a goatee and blue eyes was invited into the President's study.

"Mr. President," Goughenbaugh began, "I appreciate your not embarrassing Dr. Trench in front of the media."

"Never intended to, Talmage. But I have my own sources, and I know a little about medicine myself."

"Of course you do, Sir. I do, however, want to say that Dr. Trench is very respected."

"No one's questioning that," Porter said. "Sit down. Let's not be formal about this."

The Health and Human Services Secretary took a chair beside the President's desk.

"Now," Porter said, "speak your piece."

"It's just that your comments about masks — and hydroxychloroquine. They are directly opposed to the CDC's recommendations."

"No, they're merely alternatives. And I understand that puts pressure on the CDC. But I don't want the American public to follow a pied piper like blind mice. Medicine and science have many disagreements. There's no such thing as a one-size-fits-all answer for many things. I want people to make up their minds by themselves. The CDC does not have a corner on the truth. In fact, according to Dr. Trench — who hasn't treated patients since her internship after she first received her MD — they don't have any clinically active in her office. And they have refused to accept input from doctors who have successfully treated patients with COVID. She promised me that she is going to begin a study with physicians who are using HCQ — today."

"What about the future, Mr. President? Should the CDC back off and not take the lead in this pandemic?"

"Absolutely not. That's the role I expect from them. But I don't want them or the public to get the idea that words from the CDC are written in stone and handed to them by God. For example, I think they are dead wrong about this whole mask thing, and I've said my piece about that. They are also at least remiss not to have considered HCQ and the other medications I mentioned for treating COVID. It makes them look incompetent when they close themselves off to one and only one approach."

Porter sat back in his desk chair. "Talmage, I admire the fact that you are here this morning, standing up for your people. Make sure they know it. But also make sure that they listen to all opinions — particularly proven and validated opinions. I want us to be leading the world on this thing. And the CDC can't do that if they're keeping one eye on Big Pharma and thinking about what's good for them. While some doctors over there may well already be in the pockets of Pfizer, J & J, Bristol-Myers Squibb, GlaxoSmithKline, or any of the others — their job is to serve the American public. So is mine. What I expect from your people is thoughtful but informed guidance. I will be looking over their shoulders with my input. And if I think they are missing something or headed in the wrong direction, I will let them know. I won't challenge them in public — as I didn't with Dr. Trench. But I do want everyone at the CDC to know I expect nothing but the best from them."

Talmage Goughenbaugh got to his feet.

"Thank you, Mr. President. I'll ensure that we're all on the same page from now on."

Porter stood, too.

"Thank you, Talmage. I appreciate your directness and your having the backs of your people."

❦

❦

That afternoon, back in the Oval Office, Porter met with Inez Ceely, Ella Suzuki, and Ward Adair. Graham Newcome was also in attendance.

The White House Congressional Liaison, Ms. Ceely, was a medium dark-skinned lady known for her colorful turtleneck sweaters. She was wearing a knitted solid purple sweater under a teal jacket and matching pleated skirt.

Ella Suzuki favored pink and wore a scoop-necked sweater with emerald green slacks.

Ward Adair, buzz-cut white-blond hair, blotchy skin, was fit, and it showed through his dress shirt. He spoke to Inez, "How are we doing up on the hill?"

"Viagra jokes are making the rounds."

"Of course," Ella said.

"A couple of them are funny," Porter said with a smile. "At least they're not making war on us today."

"The independents are the audience for most of these jokes — some of which they've heard a couple of times. But they're taking them with good humor — and lowering the antagonism they usually face. But, Mr. President, if you're looking to introduce some legislation, none of the Independents are strong enough yet."

"Then who?" Porter asked. "I want someone to notice that the vast majority of our medications come from overseas. So in the event of an emergency — not just this pandemic — but God forbid a shooting war — we are at the mercy of others. Not a place I want us to be."

Ella said, "That's something the Democrats, the Republicans, and the Independents can get behind."

"But who can carry the ball?" Porter looked to his Congressional Liaison.

"I'm thinking, Greg Montgomery," she answered after only a moment's thought. "Tea Party, but jovial and well-liked."

"Junior Senator from South Dakota," Ward said, squinting as if he were scrolling through a Congressional Rolodex in his mind. "That's good. And to start this in the Senate is also a good idea. I think we can even get a Democrat to co-sponsor such a bill."

"What we need," Porter said, sitting forward and leaning his forearms on his legs, "is a measure that incentivizes Big Pharma to build plants over here."

"We could easily make that attractive," Ella volunteered. "Some local tax rebates — and a willing workforce from the Midwest rust belt."

"That's the kind of thing we need," the President said.

Inez Ceely picked up her phone and scrolled through a list of contacts. "There could be a half dozen Senators who would love to be associated with such a bill."

"Let's look at who's going to be up for reelection first." Ward was always the most practical of the President's political team. "Nothing says 'Vote For Me' like bringing in new business to the state with plenty of jobs."

"I suggest we get Felix Alvarez to draft the bill, and Inez can see that Senator Montgomery gets it," Ella suggested. Alvarez was a well-connected DC lawyer and deal maker.

"Then a day or two later, let some possible co-sponsors just happen to come across it," Inez grinned.

"Well," Porter said, "that didn't take long."

CHAPTER 27

The badge he flashed at her wasn't real. It read Special Agent and was penned to the inside of a thin, two-sided black leather wallet. The facing side had the printed name of Owen Perrymore under a plastic cover. Over the other information on the ID, all of which was false, as were the blue embossed word "OFFICIAL across the whole thing."

"Ms. Jalee Durward?" the man in the black suit, white shirt, and black tie asked, showing her his credentials.

She swallowed and answered in a quiet voice, "Yes." At twenty-two, Jalee was diminutive in every sense. Slender and coltish, her mousy brown hair was straight and hung down her back below her shoulder blades. Her complexion was delicate, her face softly sculpted, her eyes dove gray with sweeping eyelashes, and she had a cute upturned nose.

"I'd like to speak with you — privately — for a few minutes," he said.

She swallowed again and said nothing as she pushed open the glass outside door and stepped back inside.

As he came into her brick row townhouse in a middle-class neighborhood of Broken Bow, Oklahoma, she saw the black briefcase he was carrying. She didn't close the inside front door but left it open, letting the morning sunshine in.

"I am Special Agent Owen Perrymore," he said. The man was in his thirties — easily over six feet tall, with dark auburn hair and an open face. Something about the man put her at ease. She sensed she had nothing to fear from him. He crossed to the couch and stood behind a coffee table facing a modest forty-two-inch big screen TV. "I'd like to show you some pictures and ask you a few questions. May I sit down?"

"Please do," Jalee said. She wore a black skirt and white blouse with a tan Choctaw Casino vest and a black name tag with white letters. She had just come home from an overnight shift where she dealt blackjack.

He sat down, unbuttoned his jacket, and put his briefcase on her coffee table. She sat in a padded armchair with her back to the curtained front window.

"We are trying to build a case against Irving Zaddach," he said, opening his briefcase.

At the mention of Zaddach's name, she cupped her mouth with her right hand.

"You are in no legal jeopardy, Ms. Durward. In fact, we believe you to be a victim. That's why we're asking for your help."

Jalee swallowed again and closed her eyes for a moment without removing her hand covering her mouth. When she opened her eyes, she saw that he had extracted a manila folder from inside his briefcase.

He thumbed through some papers and pulled out a group of eight by ten color photographs. The Vice President's man moved his briefcase to one side and put the stack of pictures out on the end of the coffee table near Jalee.

"Would you please look through these pictures and tell me if this is you in these pictures?"

Slowly she reached for the eight by tens, and a shiver went through her. In the pictures were a younger Jalee Durward in the lap of middle-aged men, men with an arm around her waist pulling her to them, or getting into a hot tub or swimming pool in a bikini.

She closed her eyes again and clenched her teeth as tears streamed down her face.

"How old were you when these pictures were taken?" the man calling himself Owen Perrymore asked quietly.

She managed to open her eyes again and saw the man on her couch was offering her a clean white handkerchief. She accepted his offered cloth and wiped her face, and dabbed at her tears until they stopped.

When she spoke, it was quietly — ashamedly. "Fourteen — fifteen."

"Do you know who these men are?"

"Some of them," she said and paused while she pulled out two other pictures in the group. She said, "And these are Irv." She handed the selected pictures back to the man. "And these," she pulled out two more, "have Seeley in them."

"Seeley?" the man asked.

"Seeley Caruso. She was Irv's girlfriend — assistant — and finder."

"You mean she found girls like you for Zaddack?"

"Yes."

Jalee took a couple of breaths. And then say said, "She trained us — got us ready for Irv — and then for the others."

The Vice President's man studied the pictures of a slender, mildly attractive woman in her early thirties.

"So she groomed you to be with Zaddack and the others."

The young woman nodded her head.

"Are you aware that it is a crime for under-aged girls like you to have non-consensual sex with older men?"

She took a deep breath and looked Agent Perrymore in the eyes. "It wasn't non-consensual. I didn't want it — but I never said 'No.' Not to any of them."

"It's still a crime, Ms. Durward. And the fact Zaddack and this woman Seeley Caruso groomed you for it makes it more so. You — and the other girls — on the island and in the house in New York — are all victims."

"I am so ashamed," she said, bowing her head and crying again. "When I got away from there — I swore I'd never do anything like that again. I don't even have a boyfriend. I don't trust anyone that way." She cried some more. It was only after she had stopped and wiped her face with his handkerchief again that she could say, "I've tried to push all of it out of my mind — out of my life. It hurts so much to even think about it."

"Do you realize that there are other girls this is happening to — right now? Zaddack and Seeley are still doing it. And they won't stop until someone steps forward and calls them out."

"You mean, go public? Testify?"

"Yes," he said gently. "We can get you some help. For so long, this thing you've carried is not something you need to suffer from anymore. But unless someone is brave enough to stand up to them — it will go on and on and on."

"But why does it have to be me?"

"You're not the only victim we're talking to, Ms. Durward. But the more witnesses — the more *victims* we can get — the sooner we can stop this — and the worse we can see that the punishment is."

They sat in silence for several minutes. Jalee cried again. When she appeared to have run out of tears, she looked up with a clenched jaw. "I'll testify," she said with resolve and even anger.

He took back the rest of the pictures, put them in his briefcase, and closed it. When he stood, she did too.

"We're going to assign a team to watch over you. You won't see them, but they'll be there."

"Thank you," she said after giving this idea some thought.

"First, if you need to ask for some time off from your job — they'll give you no hassle about it. If you like, we can get a qualified counselor to help you come to terms with what has happened. A Special attorney'll contact you. We'll need you to give a recorded deposition. All of this will remain confidential until we are ready to prefer charges. If you have any questions," he said as he handed her a card with the name Owen Perrymore and the title Special Agent. A phone number was at the bottom. "You can call this number anytime, night or day."

She nodded her head again and fell in behind him when he went to the door.

As he stepped out, she said again, "Thank you."

"We thank *you*, Ms. Durward. You are doing a brave thing here."

"No, I mean, thank you for making me face up to this. I've tried to hide from it as long as I can. It's time I grew up and did what I know I should have done years ago."

CHAPTER 28

In late May, in an abandoned Duluth, Minnesota mall, a group of homeless squatters confronted a security guard hired by the property owner. When the guard, twenty-nine-year-old Tyrus White, ordered the trespassers to leave, he was attacked. He was hit with thrown glass bottles and stones to hold occupants' tents to the floor. White pulled his pistol, a 9mm Glock 17, and fired three rounds. The crowd scattered, but one slug struck and killed a fifty-eight-year-old homeless crack addict, Marcus Taylor. Both men were black.

By the second night, Duluth became the latest BLM and ANTIFA-led protest scene. The event developed into a looting and burning melee in the city's center. It was well beyond the ability of the Duluth police — even with the help of officers from neighboring Superior, Wisconsin.

Duluth is the world's farthest inland port accessible to oceangoing ships. It is the largest and busiest port on the Great Lakes. It forms a metropolitan area with Superior, Wisconsin. Together, they are called the Twin Ports. Both are situated on the north shore of Lake Superior and the westernmost point of the Great Lakes.

It was a hub for tourism and cargo shipping before it became the site of violence and unlawful behavior.

Duluth is home to eighty-six thousand, making it Minnesota's fifth-largest city and the center of Minnesota's second-largest metropolitan area. Together, the Twin Ports have a population of close to two-hundred-eighty thousand.

The signs and posters of the protest/riot proclaimed the usual BLM slogans, 'Black Lives Matter," and "Defund The Police," but added, "White Kills Black - Again," "Justice For Marcus," and calls for "Critical Race Theory."

CRT, as it is known, is an outgrowth of the European Marxist school of "critical theory." Critical race theory is a semi-scholarly movement that links race, racism, and power. Based on a little-known book by the same name, the ideas are to challenge and overturn the very foundations of Western civilization. Rationalism, constitutional law, and legal reasoning are rejected as white-privilege constructs.

Unlike the Civil Rights movement at the beginning of the 1960s, which sought to work within the structures of democracy, critical race theorists argue that Western social life, political structures, and economic systems are founded upon racism. It is a theory of black victimhood. Reparations, black preferences for every sector of society, lower academic standards for blacks, and history taught to all from a black victim perspective are key elements of the theory.

Porter called Duluth mayor Elenor Rayner at 2 AM Central Time, 1 AM Eastern.

"Mr. President?" the voice of the 50-something lady came over the speaker on the President's desk in the Oval Office.

"Mrs. Rainer," Porter responded. "This is President Randall. I'm calling you from the White House. Is there anything we can do for you?"

"Thank you, Mr. President," Mayor Rainer said. "I just got off the phone with Governor Olson. He has called out the National Guard. They should be here in the morning."

"Good," Porter said. "What is happening there now?"

"Our Chief of Police says two busloads of protesters arrived an hour ago. He says people, who live near where the busses are parked, told him they unloaded printed signs, five-gallon plastic jugs — no one knows what is in them — helmets, backpacks, and things like bats with nails in them. The looters have smashed windows, storefronts, lit piles of tires on fires in the street, and have carried out TVs, clothing, and jewelry from stores they have attacked."

"Has anyone been injured?"

"A couple of police officers have been — but not seriously. We have moved the security guard who did the shooting, out of the city."

"Wise," Porter said.

"We have some State Troopers and some horse-riding police officers who are holding a line at one intersection. I don't think they'll be overrun."

"All right. If there comes a time or if you decide you are not getting the help you need from your governor, please call me. And I mean that."

"I believe you, Mr. President. And I also understand how you are restrained from doing much. But at this moment, I think we will have a handle on this by tomorrow. I will call if not. Thank you for taking the time to think about us."

"It is the least I can do. I'd like to do more — and will if you feel a need."

"Thank you, Mr. President."

"Goodbye, Madam Mayor."

"The President's next call was to Minnesota Governor Wiley Olson.

The summer was hot, and the Climate Change crowd came out in force. Their chief advocates flew their private planes to major conferences in Paris, Dubai, and Pretoria, South Africa. The summer heat was evidence to all in attendance of what these people once called Global Warming. However, when science disproved this with data, showing instead the world was headed toward a new Ice Age in the next thousand years, the movement adopted the "Climate Change" as their moniker and catchphrase.

Protest evolved into riots across the US. At times, these rampages needed little provocation. In New Jersey, a traffic stop for speeding ignited a two-day event. Police became hesitant to enforce the laws aggressively, and crimes of all sorts grew. Cities saw the quickest and fastest rise in crime, where police budgets were cut in response to protest/riot demands.

The new call was for "no bail." Progressive cities with liberal mayors and like-minded District Attorneys adopted such measures. This turned police stations into a revolving door for an expanding class of criminals. Some DAs went as far as announcing what they called "non-violent" offenses that they would not prosecute. A dollar limit was even placed on shoplifted items, making those crimes de facto no longer crimes.

A pattern of elected officials who had received significant campaign contributions and other forms of support from multi-billionaire Jerren Glowicki came to light. Also backed by Glowicki, state legislatures passed lenient laws signed by governors. These new laws contributed to a rise in homelessness, public-funded drug treatment facilities, which were, in fact, little more than taxpayer-supported drug dens.

Additional results were low morale among the police ranks and difficulty hiring new personnel. Lack of vigorous enforcement, in turn, contributed to the rise in crime.

Porter spoke out on these issues in his weekly podcasts. Howard Sterling echoed and defended the President's remarks in his daily White House Press Briefings. However, the media's prime focus was still COVID and the appearance of Dr. Trench.

CHAPTER 29

Of the other six women on David Royal's — or Special Agent Owen Perrymore's list, three agreed to do as Jalee Durward had done. They would give recorded depositions and testify in court. Two of the others had committed suicide, and one was working in the porn film business. She wasn't considered an excellent open court witness because of her life choices after getting away from Irving Zaddach.

Royal returned to Vice President Holyoak's office. Again, he came by the DC underground tunnel system and the secret passageway behind the VP's study. And once more, he was in a military uniform with the rank and name tag of Lt. Colonel Givens. He delivered printed copies of the recorded depositions of the four women he had collected. The VP took the folder he handed her, and Royal left.

Vice President Holyoak asked the President's personal secretary, Ms. Gwendolyn Jacobs, to schedule her a half-hour with the President whenever it was convenient.

"I apologize for putting something else on your plate, Mr. President," she said when she was slotted into the Oval Office for their meeting and handed Porter the folder.

The VP waited in Porter's office while he read the depositions. The

President was both shocked and disgusted with what he learned. Sitting back in his chair at his desk in the Oval Office, he slowly shook his head and tightened his jaw.

"What do you need?" he asked Tracy.

"A FISA surveillance warrant."

The Foreign Intelligence Surveillance Court – or FISA — is housed in a windowless room in a secure area of the US District Court on Constitution Avenue. Government officials had never revealed the precise location. The court comprises eleven judges who sit for seven-year terms. All are federal district judges who have agreed to take on the additional duties rotating. Each judge is appointed by the Chief Justice of the Supreme Court.

"Give me a couple of days," Porter said. "I'll have to talk to the Attorney General. With the new director at the FBI, I'm not sure if they should be involved or not."

"I'll leave that to you, Mr. President. The man you don't know about is ready to deploy where he thinks he can get the best evidence."

"I understand," Porter said.

"I think everybody needs to play this close to the vest until we're ready to make arrests."

"Agreed. I'll make sure everyone I talk to gets it."

"Thank you for your time, Sir," Tracy said before leaving the President's office.

The Attorney General had been cleared, and Porter was glad. He trusted Hamilton Stockman. The career federal prosecutor from Kansas had come to the President's attention during the trial of sophisticated and nationwide drug smugglers operating out of Manhattan, Kansas.

The man who sat on the Oval Office couch across from Porter was 40 and considered young for the office. The youngest US Attorney General had been Richard Rush — the 8th US AG at thirty-five. He served under President Madison. Robert Kennedy was only one year older when he served in the office under his brother, John F. Kennedy.

Hamilton Stockman had thin blonde eyebrows over light moss-green eyes. He parted his thick hair on the left side of his angular face. He was a pleasant-looking man who spoke with a deep, resonant voice.

After reading over the depositions, he looked up at the President.

"My God, I hope we can put a stop to this creep, Irving Zaddach, and his girlfriend. But I have a feeling there's more involved than just sex with underaged girls."

"Very perceptive," Porter said. "But I'm not sure what it is. That's why we need a FICA full surveillance warrant."

The Fourth Amendment protects against unreasonable searches. Therefore, a warrant is always required regardless of what type of surveillance was needed by law enforcement.

"I believe I can get that. However, Mr. President, I'm not sure if the FBI's ready to take point on this. I've had some talks with Konner Ochoa. He has to do more of a house cleaning than he first thought."

The President smiled as he said, "People suddenly want to spend more time with their families and take early retirement?"

"That's what he's telling me. However, we may see some of them back with charges against them. And he says it's still a very leaky ship."

"Then we don't want them. I think when Konner gets through, the FBI will be what we always used to think it was."

"Agreed," the Attorney General said. "My opinion is that we appoint a Special Prosecutor."

"Can we do that without generating a lot of smoke?"

"No, Sir. Let me rethink that." Hamilton Stockman only had to think a moment before he said, "I like the broad powers a Special Prosecutor has, but I know some US attorneys who can get the job done — on the down-low — until it's time to go public."

"Then find one and let's go that way," Porter said. "And," the President went on after a moment, "there is someone already on this case — someone to be trusted but not to be known. I can't even divulge his identity to you, Hamilton. It's not for lack of trust in you — but there are other factors at play."

"Then I won't ask, Mr. President."

"He's the one who sought out these women and got them to give depositions. And I don't even know his name."

"Whatever you say. But what's his forte?"

"James Bond."

"Got ya'."

"He'll bring anything he gets to us."

"Couldn't ask for more. Anything else I need to know?"

"I don't think so."

Hamilton stood with the folder in his hands. "Then I'll get on with this and keep you in the loop."

"Thank you, Hamilton."

"Whatever you need, Mr. President."

CHAPTER 30

The number of infections continued on a rocket rise. There was much public debate about mask-wearing. Since President Randall's outspoken lack of support for them, there was a divide among American citizens about the efficacy and need for masks. Those who masked, and public officials, from governors to mayor and town councils who mandated face coverings, caused some incidents in restaurants and airplanes.

Embarrassed politicians became the mocking target of social media memes when they were caught and photographed, disregarding their own rules. The phrase, "Rules for thee but not for me," became a popular response. Supposedly high-minded officials blatantly seem to discard their demands. They treated masking as a needless inconvenience and were mocked for it.

Howard asked the correspondent at a Press Briefing and the public to check the boxes from which their masks came. "Most," he said, "will discover Made In China printed on the containers. How much do you think you should be relying for your protection on a product from the country which gave us the virus in the first place?"

American and foreign face masks began making them with political, commercial, and humorous designs. Regardless of the President's position, there was money to be made from those who believed every utterance of the CDC.

Dr. Sinead Trench asked for a meeting in the Oval Office with the President on a September afternoon before the daily Press Briefing. Dr. Trench came supported by her colleagues, Dr. Judson Whitehead, whom the President still thought of as the Muppet "Beaker," and Dr. Laurennie Jarry. Even Secretary of Health and Human Services, Talmage Goughenbaugh, was in attendance.

The three physicians took one couch, and Secretary Goughenbaugh shared the other with Porter's Chief-of-Staff, Graham Newcome, and Darla Ritter, the VP's Chief-of-Staff. Porter took his usual chair at one end of the couches beside a coffee table. The Vice President sat in the other chair beside the President.

"I see you came loaded for bear," Porter said when everyone was seated. "Let's cut to the chase."

Dr. Trench handed out a sheet of paper with the latest infections numbers and deaths. She gave the President a moment to absorb the figures and the graph of anticipated cases and deaths.

"As you can see, Mr. President, this pandemic is growing at an alarming rate — not just here, but worldwide. We're also experiencing a spike in deaths. We have been discussing this and feel it is time to call for some drastic measures."

"Drastic — like what?"

"We would like to call for at least a pause in possible spreader events. These would include mass concerts, festivals, sporting events, cruise ship cruises — and even family gatherings — any celebratory events. In fact, any gathering of three or more people."

"Religious services? I seem to remember a Bible quote that read something like — Whenever two or three of you are gathered in My name, I will be with you.' How about protests?" Porter asked. "Would you want to pause them?"

"We don't feel as if political events should be our purview," Dr. Trench said. "We are not trying to prevent any citizen from exercising their Constitutional rights."

"It seems to me that's exactly what you are doing," the President said. "Particularly their religious rights." Then after a pause when no one responded to his statement, Porter said, "And how long do you propose such a halt? You realize you're talking about asking people to not go to work — closing businesses — in effect having everyone 'shelter in place.' And I hope you are calling for a pause in those, too."

"Of course, Mr. President," Dr. Trench suddenly didn't like being the voice for the CDC. There was silence in the Oval Office a few moments until Dr. Trench sat up straight and said, "Two weeks. Two weeks to slow the spread."

"And after that?"

"We believe it is time to restrict movement, travel, and shopping — to some extent."

"You want to close grocery stores? Filling stations? Doctors and dentist's offices? Schools? Even Congress?"

"We have a list of what we think are 'essential' businesses." She offered another sheet of paper to everyone.

"So Congress is essential — and so are several big-box stores — but mom and pop businesses, in fact, most businesses, you want to close. Churches, Synagogues. For weeks — now — but then you'll want to extend it — for months? Even maybe a year?"

"We understand this is drastic, Mr. President," Dr. Trenched stressed.

"It's not just drastic — it's Draconian! It would kill businesses."

"And many people along the way who are not even sick," VP Tracy Holyoak added.

"We don't know of any other way to stop this virus from spreading, Mr. President."

"I have heard no one talk about effective treatments — or a vaccine?" Porter said.

"Mr. President, we are still studying your hydroxchloroquine protocol."

"How about the others?"

"We do tentatively support the five-day treatment course of ivermectin. We have encouraged mass testing and COVID case tracking."

"How about Remdesivir? Hospitalization of high-risk patients was reduced by 89% when Remdesivir is given in the first few days after symptoms appeared."

"That has been reported but has not been proven?" Dr. Trench was trying not to be confrontational. "But even in the reports, the best results have come from its use in a hospital setting. That simply isn't available for everyone."

"And a vaccine?"

"Mr. President, as a doctor, you know it takes three to seven years to get any new medication through the system."

"Then let's cut the time to the bone. And cut the regulations," he said to his Vice President. "A vaccine could be worth millions to any company that can produce a proven one. Let's call it FTL and get the development going. I'm sure Big Pharma has some possibilities in the pipeline."

"What's FTL?" Dr. Trench asked.

"It's a science fiction term meaning faster than light," Porter answered.

"What do we do until one of the companies comes up with something?" Dr. Trench asked.

Porter sat back and thought a moment, glancing over at Tracy and Graham. Finally, he sat up and said, "Two weeks to slow the spread."

There was a noticeable sigh from the physicians.

"But," Porter warned, "I want to see data on this every day. And understand, this is a suggestion — only a suggestion — it's not an order — or a mandate. I don't have the power to do that, and neither do you — or anyone else. This is still a representative republic — not a dictatorship."

"Yes, Sir," Dr. Trench said, looking around at her colleagues. "May we also announce your — F-T-L proposal?"

"Definitely," Porter said and paused. "But I want you and everyone to understand I am not endorsing any vaccine yet to be produced. I'm willing to give you odds that whatever comes out will only be experimental. I'll have to study it well before I get injected — with anything."

Porter got to his feet, and everyone else followed.

"Thank you for your time, Mr. President," Dr. Trench said as she put on her face mask and left to the Press Briefing Room.

CHAPTER 31

Porter stopped and talked to the mostly masked press as he and First Lady were leaving for a weekend back in Amarillo.

"Mr. President," Irish Leftwich, the MSNBC White House reporter, called out. "Aren't you setting a terrible example for the public by not wearing a mask?"

"Do some research," Porter answered. "Read the studies on cloth and paper masks. Report on what you find."

"So, you are following the science?" South African reporter Steve Odili asked.

"Science is a search for the truth. It is never — 'the truth.' The CDC disagrees with me. Out of an abundance of caution, they recommended masking. They also recommended this 'two weeks to stop the spread.' But those are recommendations — not laws. I think most people will go along with the CDC — but the American public is made up of people and not sheep. We are all still free to follow the recommendations or not."

"Are you going to your ranch?" another reporter called out.

"We are."

"Are you going to isolate there for two weeks?"

"I am happy to isolate with the First Lady any chance we get."

Porter looked over at Deidra, who smiled and chuckled. Back to the gathered reporters on the South Lawn of the White House, he said, "But it won't be for two weeks. We need a break — but even there, I'm on the job. This is a twenty-four-hour, seven-days-a-week, three-hundred-sixty-five-days-a-year job."

Demona Enock, the strawberry blonde from WOLF Cable News, called out, "Are you supporting the American Made Medication bill in Congress?"

"It sounds like a good idea to me. I'll have to see what comes out of it."

"What are your reactions to the events in Duluth?"

"The security guard — who is black — was attacked. His last name is White. He's not Caucasian. Those signs saying 'White Kills Black" were just wrong. They are meant to stir up racial division and hatred. Looting and burning businesses are not a protest. Those are the acts of criminals."

"Is it true that you called the mayor of Duluth?"

"I did. And the governor. They appeared to have a handle on the situation."

"Would you have sent in troops?" another reporter asked.

"I wasn't asked. But like Ike did in Little Rock, and Herbert Hoover did with the Bonus Army here in DC back in 1932, I will do whatever is needed."

With that, Porter turned and linked arms with the First Lady. They boarded the marine Osprey, Marine One, and lifted off.

The trial for Portland Officer Bent Song, began. The fifth-generation Chinese/American patrol police officer charged with the murder of three-hundred-pound bully, drug and alcohol abuser, Michael Robertson.

Although body camera footage showed Robertson bull-rushing the officer after repeated verbal warnings, the Portland District Attorney charged the young officer with capital murder. The DA Iola Found was a multi-billionaire Jerren Glowicki supported candidate for the office.

The attractive twenty-nine-year-old black woman looked good on camera and clearly articulated her ultra-liberal ambitions. As a prosecutor, she used BLM and CRT ideas at every opportunity. The sequestered jury was split by the second day of the trial. This was when the whole panel of doxed — their names, photographs, addresses, and phone numbers were published on social media. Everything changed when the jury got word of this, a note being slipped to the jury foreperson by a court bailiff.

The jury quickly rethought what looked like a straightforward case of a police officer doing his duty and being forced to defend himself. By the end of final arguments, the case had turned into "an unprovoked and racially inspired killing," as DA Iola Found described the event.

With less than three hours of deliberation, the panel returned a verdict of first-degree murder. While Officer Song's defense team called for a mistrial, the judge overruled the argument, and a sentencing date was set for the following week.

The trial judge, who had welcomed cameras into the courtroom and had gladly given TV and radio interviews both before and during the trial, was doxed and threatened, too. Intimidation worked. The judge sentenced Song to life in prison.

What shocked the nation was that Bent Song was given a Presidential pardon before he ever reached the prison. At Porter's suggestion, Attorney General Hamilton Stockman put Officer Song into Witsec — an acronym for Witness Protection Program. This US Marshal-run program saw to the release and movement of Song, his wife, and child. Secretary of the Interior, Linton Ston, found a Park Ranger position for Song, at Mt. Denali National Park in Alaska.

Porter took to the Press Briefing Room's podium to explain his actions. Showing the camera footage used in the trial and recorded witness testimony for the televised trial, the President asked any reporter to dispute the visual evidence or the words of Portland residents who knew Michael Robertson to be a bully and addict.

"I took this action after watching the trial myself, and knowing the social media doxing of the jury and the judge. Thirteen-hundred Pennsylvania Avenue is my address. Anyone who has a problem with my action already knows where I live."

The questions from the media were weak and gutless. Porter had no trouble answering them and defending his action. He ended by quoting Abraham Lincoln.

"All I can do is the best that I can do. If the end brings me out all right, what is said against me won't amount to anything. If the end brings me out wrong, then ten angels swearing I was right would make no difference."

With that, Porter left the room.

CHAPTER 32

One of the most-watched YouTube videos was of an up-and-coming young comic named Wally Cornfield. He had dark hair which hung straight to his shoulders. Cornfield had a handsome, sculpted face with dark eyes and a wide grin. He wore wide horizontal striped shirts and jeans without holes. The young man walked onto a small stage with different-sized cardboard boxes glued to a gray wooden plank background. He picked up the wireless mic off the mic stand to the audience's polite applause.

"Good evening. Is everybody sober tonight?"

This got a small laugh.

"Of course, you're sober. This is Provo. Anybody got a hidden flask of Red Bull hidden away?"

The response to this line was scattered laughter, but nothing enthusiastic.

"Wrong crowd.

"My name is Wally Cornfield — and no, that doesn't mean I was conceived during an episode of Hee Haw. Actually, I'm Indian. People never know how to take that. I know you're all wondering, 'does he mean he plays the tom-tom, or he's in computer tech support?'"

The audience got a good laugh out of that line.

"Let me put it this way, my folks didn't come over on the Mayflower — but they were here to welcome them ashore. My name is Wohali — that's pronounced woh-HAH-lee — Cornfield. My friends — both of them — call me Wally. Wally Cornfield. In Cherokee, my first name means 'eagle.' In grade school, my Indian classmates — out of respect — called me 'bird brain.'"

This got the audience on Wally's side.

"I know you can't tell it by lookin', but I went to college. An aerospace engineering major. But I flunked out after two years. I kept saying there were three genders — male — female — and progressives. To me, that wasn't rocket science. I guess it was a trick question.

"My parents were really proud of me when I started college. Now that I'm a comedian, they won't even talk to me. The last thing my mother told me was I missed too many chances to shut the heck up.

"But here I am. I think I'm a success. The top of my profession. I've come a long way from Tahlequah, Oklahoma. Look at me now — here I am right across the street from a Walgreens — in Provo, Utah. Nobody ever thought I'd make it.

"I'm trying to follow in the footsteps of another famous Cherokee funny man. Anyone ever heard of Will Rogers?"

Everyone clapped at this.

"Yes, Will Rogers is famous for saying, 'I don't make jokes, I just watch the government and report the facts.' Well, that's kind of what I do, too.

"Course in Will's day, he'd just read to folks out of the newspapers. Nowadays, nobody reads the newspapers. And if you repeat what the reporters say on TV, they'll sue you for character assassination. They'll say nobody is stupid enough to say the things they've said. And you play them the video of it, and they claim it's been doctored. I say they should have been doctored before they ever went on air. As the ranchers say, 'Castration makes for a gentle horse.'

"I see where Congress has designated itself an 'essential business.' There is so much wrong with that. Talk about your oxymorons. How can you use the words Congress in the same sentence as 'essential'?

"Well, I guess you could say Congress moves like an oxcart full of morons.

THE IMPEACHED PRESIDENT

"Hey, don't laugh at me. You're the ones who elected them.

"Congress — that's the life. Three-day work weeks — and that's when they're in session — which is only between holidays. At the moment, they're in recess? We're in a pandemic, and they're in recess. You remember recess; you used to go outside and play with your friends? When was the last time Congress was outside? Or had friends? Congress doesn't have friends. They have sponsors — like golfers and NASCAR drivers. I just wish they put the patches on their clothes. Then we'd know who they were really representing.

"The politicians in DC like the idea of wearing a mask all the time. Like the President said, they're not going to perform surgery. Who would trust these clowns with a scalpel? But they are holding us up like a convenience store.

"Taxes — that they love. Their new motto should be 'More taxes — for thee — but not for me.'

"And income taxes have made liars out of more of us than fishing or golf.'

"Maybe that's why some people get into politics — they're good at lyin' and getting away with it on their income tax.

"You know the old saying — a fool and their corporate money are soon elected.

"Are we going to continue to put up with this? It's like Will Rogers once said, 'There are three kinds of men. The one that learns by reading. The few who learn by observation. The rest of them have to pee on the electric fence for themselves.'

"I think I've got the second-best job in the country. Heck, I've got all the politicians in all the parties writing material for me — every day.

"The best job in the country has to be being vice-president. All she has to do is get up in the morning and say, 'How is the president doing today?'

"Now, I like President Randall. Do you?"

The audience bursts into the loudest applause of the comic's set.

"He's got common sense. And that one thing you can't legislate. And I don't think Congress would even try."

This brought more applause than laughter.

"The more I watch politicians, the more I think each party is worse than the other.

"It's gotten to the point where the only difference between death and taxes is death doesn't get worse every time Congress meets."

"Just be thankful we're not getting all the government we're actually paying for. But we have the best Congress money can buy — the thing is — it wasn't us that bought 'em.

"Think of all the money we spend on government — and it's not one bit better than the one we had for one-third the money ten years ago.

"And the media isn't any better. They don't know the truth from a corporate paycheck. If they ever injected truth into politics, it would ruin politics.

"Today, our Congress wouldn't pass the Ten Commandments — at least without giving themselves a get-out-of-hell free card.

"I believe the country has come this far despite politics — not because of it.

"My old man told me he could remember back when a progressive was someone who was generous with his money.

"Remember, Ancient Rome declined because it had a Senate. What are our chances? We have both a House and a Senate?

"It's not what politicians don't know that hurts. It's what they know that just ain't so."

This line always drew a big laugh for him.

"Ronald Reagan said that. I have to give him credit.

"I will say this for the Senate — it always opens with a prayer — but it also always closes with an investigation. And the truth is, government investigations have contributed more to our amusement than they have to our knowledge.

"How about we declare one day a year — just one — when it's open season on politicians? Talk about cleaning up the swamp.

"But it's our fault. When was the last time you voted *for* something and not just *against* something or someone else?

"The way things seem to work in DC, they should legalize every crime and then tax it out of business. Am I wrong?

"Americans are very generous people. And we'll forgive almost any weakness — with the possible exception of stupidity. But then — every couple of years, we tend to elect a lot of that.

"I've thought about it and decided that instead of giving money to fund colleges and trade schools — to promote learning — why don't we pass a constitutional amendment prohibiting anybody from learning anything? If it works as well as the Prohibition amendment did, we'd be the most intelligent people on earth in a few years.

"A couple of things to remember. First — socialism is like prohibition — it sounds like a good idea, but it just doesn't work.

"Second — there is no income tax in China. But there's no income there either.

"Thirdly — once somebody holds public office, they are absolutely no good anymore for honest work.

"And lastly — don't be like Congress — the kind of people who spend money they haven't earned, to buy things they don't want, to impress people they don't even like.

"I'm Wally Cornfield! Good night!"

CHAPTER 33

A ghillie suit is the sniper's best friend. The word ghillie comes from Scottish mythology. Ghillie Dhu was a fairy clothed in leaves and moss.

The first known use of ghillie suits was during the 1916 Second Boer War in Africa. The Lovat Scouts, a Scottish Highlands regiment, began recruiting men from Scottish Highlands estates. Gamekeepers and professional game stalkers were the men the military sought. Of particular interest were men from Gairloch, where the tale of Ghillie Dhu originated.

The Boer Wars, I and II, were fought between the British and Dutch settlers of the South African Transvaal, a province of South Africa north of the Vaal River. The Dutch were known as "Boers" — their word for "farmer."

To David Royal, all that mattered was that his ghillie suit made him all but invisible on Irving Zaddach's Caribbean island. He lay in the foliage of the Big Breast Island. In the Bermuda island chain, East of Cuba, North of Haiti, and the Dominican Republic. The island group occupies one-hundred-eighty square miles, East-Southeast of Miami. The chain runs from Bermuda South to the Turks and the Caicos

Islands. The Vice President's man was ready with a Sony FE 200-600MM long zoon lens. He was awaiting the arrival of the "Coed Convoy," any one of six airplanes Zaddach owned. The monthly party began when the plane touched down, and the male guests alighted. The social function was quickly underway as the young women in bikinis made themselves available to the arriving guests.

The hidden photographer began shooting as soon as a Boeing 727 lined up on the runway on the long strip of land east of one of the island's breasts. When the craft taxied and stopped, its tail number was visible. A picture was snapped and sent by a microburst to an expansive cabin cruiser five miles away.

This was not the boat the Vice President's man had used when he knocked out the island's power during a small tropical storm. That time he had slipped inside the buildings and planted digital cameras, which looked like clear silicone pads used to cushion glass top tables from their legs.

This time the yacht belonged to a billionaire friend of Billy Uker. Uker, 27, lost a leg in the Baghdad Green Zone. He worked in Army Intelligence and had warned of the upcoming attack. His superiors ignored his warning, and six people were killed. Out of the service, Uker had become a billionaire and private space company executive. His skunkworks had produced the cameras he gave to his long-time friend, David Royal.

David had asked if Uker could get a different boat for another mission? Royal's thinking was not to appear familiar to anyone on Big Breasts who might be keeping track of such things. Uker asked a fellow billionaire friend for the loan of his yacht. The friend was slowly dying from pancreatic cancer.

"Might as well," the dying man said from flat on his back in his palatial estate. "Somebody should get some use out of the thing. Go and enjoy."

The yacht was piloted by the same retired CIA agent who had helped before. He quickly outfitted the craft with recording and transmitting equipment like the buoy they'd left the last time. The buoy looked like a piece of driftwood with an almost invisible antenna. But it was on the west side of the island. The yacht was parked east of the Big Breasts this time. Also on board were two female agents David Royal had worked with before. They gladly signed on when the roll as eye candy was explained to them. The two spent their day sunbathing topless and diving off the boat to swim in the nude.

As the arrival party on the jet was met and ushered into golf carts for the trip to the island's party house, the plane was parked in a hangar. It wasn't good for the craft's interior to sit locked up out in the tropical sun. For that reason, Irving Zaddach had a temperature-controlled, multiplane hanger built. The structure was at the near end of the runway. Once parked inside and the hangar doors closed, the jet's cabin doors were left open to air out and be ready for its return flight two days away.

Back on board the pleasure boat, the retired CIA agent's computers told him the tail number matched a General Services plane awaiting parts for a repair and upgrade. A well-compensated maintenance crew chief saw that the parts were never ordered.

During the rest of the daylight, the Vice President's man moved to the other side of the Big Breast, where he had documented the plane's arrival. In his new position, he took pictures of young, topless, and sometimes naked girls frolicking in the island's seashell-shaped outdoor pool and serving drinks and drugs to the guests.

After nightfall, while the party below continued, David Royal returned to the hangar. Out of his ghillie suit, he slipped into the well-lighted metal building. At the far end of the structure, the island's guards occupied themselves with big-screen TVs, video games, and liquor. Zaddach didn't want the guards to be in evidence during his guest's party time.

David slipped in and mounted the deployed steps into the 727. He located and snapped shots of the tablet-like flight log that ran back three years. The log listed everyone on board each flight the plane had flown. Next, he got pictures of the executive cabin and the single back cabin where a wrinkled and stained round bed lay.

Late the second day, the Boeing craft was ready to take off. Again, the Vice President's man got clear shots of the party-goers as they boarded. When the plane was in the air, David made his way back to the shore. He packed his ghillie suit into a waterproof bag and slipped into the sea. He located his underwater scooter. Towing his load of gear behind him, he used the motorized machine, a night vision, and inferred guide screens to navigate his way back to the yacht.

CHAPTER 34

Congress passed The American Made Pharmaceuticals bill. However, language in the bill constituted a rider. A rider is an attachment, schedule, amendment, or other writing added to the original bill to modify it. The changes may be small or large, but in either case, the primary purpose of the rider is to avoid rewriting or redrafting the bill entirely. Riders are commonly a part of the lawmaking process in state legislatures and Congress. Riders are typically added to bills at a late stage of their evolution. The idea was to force the President to sign a bill he supported even if it were attached with language or additions he might not approve by itself.

This rider was called "The American Rescue Plan."

It authorized a payment of $1,400 for a single individual or $2,800 for a married couple and $1,400 per dependent. The language expanded qualifying dependents to include those under 19, college students under 24, and adults with disabilities. This was Congress' way of softening the nationwide shutdown.

Porter wanted to know where the money was coming from to pay for this legislation — but he didn't ask. It was a time for him to hold his nose and sign a bill. He did.

The CDC wanted to extend their recommendations of the shutdown an additional two weeks and then another month.

The nation's governors mandated the recommendations state by state. Porter questioned the power of state governments to do this, but the shutdown quickly became a worldwide phenomenon. Except for the designated "essential" businesses and workers, the world came to a halt.

The NFL season was cut in half and began halfway through November. When the truncated schedule started, there were "social justice" and BLM slogans painted on the endzones and printed on the backs of some team's helmets. Combined with the widespread kneeling during the National Anthem before games to protest against the treatment of black in America, the league saw a 19% drop in viewership and a 15% drop in ticket sales.

Churches and synagogues, as well as individuals, filed lawsuits against the mandates. By February of the new year, Florida and Texas had abandoned their lockdowns. North Dakota alone never followed the CDC shutdown recommendation after the first month.

A second round of COVID-relief legislation sent out checks of $600 for singles and $1,200 for married couples. Qualifying children also received $600 for each.

The number of COVID cases continued to rise. So did deaths attributed to the disease. The elderly were the hardest hit demographic, with children and teens to young adults having almost no reported cases or deaths.

True to Dr. Trench's predictions, refrigerated semi-truck trailers were used as holding morges in large cities like New York and Los Angeles. Images of adult children separated from ill and dying elderly parents became common on newscasts and social media posts.

The nation and the world were suffering from this pandemic. The President's weekly podcast became a staple of encouragement and hope to the US. Other world leaders tried to follow Porter's lead but ended up being more fear-mongering than inspiring.

Movements arose, questioning the CDC's advice. While the ever-present Dr. Trench was elevated to sainthood by the media, her detractors grew. It was revealed that she had given grants to the biochemical lab in Wuhan, China, to fund "gain of function" research for viruses. It was, by then, widely believed that the COVID virus had been a product of, if not purposely released by, the Wuhan lab. Dr. Trench's ties to pharmaceutical companies through stock purchases and fees for speaking engagement severely tarnished her halo.

Still, Dr. Trench advised everyone to "get tested, wash your hands regularly, stay six feet away from other people, wear a face mask — any kind of mask is better than no masks — and isolate if you develop symptoms."

Meanwhile, across the country, police officers were randomly shot and killed while sitting in patrol cars, during traffic stops, or in drive-by shootings. One statistic was suppressed by the woke mainstream media — that of the number of unarmed blacks killed by police. It was claimed that the overwhelming number of blacks killed by police was a symptom of "*systemic racism*" in American society.

A live-stream conversation with a noted mathematician, Professor Emeritus Amon Castor of MIT, was damned by BLM and social justice warriors of every kind. Dr. Castor had conducted a study to find the facts and numbers to prove or disprove assertions that the police were unfairly targeting blacks and killing them. He pointed out that the rate of black suspects shot fatally by the police was "*a function of*" how often blacks commit a crime. "Because," he said, "blacks commit most of the crime, more often than not, it's a black-on-black crime. Therefore, they have the most interactions with police."

In his study, he found that in the previous year, while African-Americans were 13% of the population, they made up 53 percent of known homicide offenders in the U.S. and committed roughly 60% of robberies. "Still," he reported, "of the 996 fatal police shootings last year, only 21 percent involved black suspects." The professor concluded that the share of black suspects shot by the police was actually "less than what the black crime rate would predict."

"The number proved," he said, "only 19 unarmed" black suspects were fatally shot by the police last year." Most liberals and progressives surveyed thought law enforcement killed 100 to 1,000 blacks annually.

The mathematician went on to say that an "*unarmed*" suspect didn't make them any less dangerous. "An unarmed suspect could still lunge at a police officer, as in the case in Portland, Oregon," Castor said, "or try to run a police officer over — or otherwise attack in a deadly fashion."

In one of his podcasts, the President observed that "America was not the hateful, racist nation some would have you believe. We are still the most open, giving, helpful, and generous people on the planet."

Then it was reported that the President had COVID. He was taken to Walter Reed Medical Center.

CHAPTER 35

Supporters gathered outside the 200 acre Walter Reed Medical Center. Known as the "President's hospital," this was where Porter had recovered from the assassination attempt during his first term as President. Porter was now given the five-day treatment course of Ivermectin. He responded well from the very beginning of the treatment. He took his limo, "the beast," out to drive by and acknowledge his supporters and well-wishers the third night he was in Walter Reed.

While he was there, the US military began its withdrawal from Afghanistan. The pullback started by drawing back troops in outlying sites. Compounds of canvas tents, mobile homes, and plywood shelters were dismantled, loaded on trucks, and taken to Bagram Air Base. There then began a steady flow of Air Force transports carrying arms, ammunition, vehicles, supplies, and personnel. The orchestrated movement first announced by Porter at the G-20 came without incident from the Taliban. The President's message and warning of "crushing response" to any Taliban interference had been conveyed to the insurgent's top leadership.

The liberal and progressive media tried to portray the withdrawal as a cowardly retreat. From his hospital bed, President Randall said,

"What is the US interest being served by this war? There is none. We have spent too much honorable blood and lives, as well as treasure, in a part of the world where we have no compelling interest. If Afghanistan is to be a united and democratic nation, it is up to its population to achieve that goal. The United States has given way more to an often unappreciated people than any have a right to expect. Nation-building is not our mission. This is not a retreat, but a withdrawal. A military operation by which our forces disengage from the enemy. We leave with honor and sadness for the price we have already paid for an ill-advised venture."

The media, which had largely denounced the Afghanistan conflict, changed their view. Commentators and reporters seemed to be committed to the war suddenly and wanted it to continue with no end in sight.

In the daily Press Briefing, Howard Sterling said simply, "Enough is enough. The US does not want to engage in endless wars. We are out of there."

Three days later, Porter returned to the White House. He took the podium in the Press Briefing Room to answer questions himself instead of putting Howard in the position of being a middleman.

"You are still not wearing a mask?" Fifty-three-year-old Miranda Bank asked from behind her mask and squinting at Porter through her horn-rimmed glasses.

"No, I'm not. You are free to report that I've not learned my lesson — but I am not contagious, and according to the Walter Reed medical staff, I now have a powerful immune response. The chances of my catching it again are point zero-nine-nine-nine percent. I'll take their word for it.

"And let's take a moment here to talk about masking. I should have gone over this before. But let's do it now.

"Are you aware that it's only been recently that the CDC *did no*t recommend wearing a face mask or covering of any kind, unless a person was known to be infected? Non-infected people have never needed to wear a mask. For example, when a person has TB, we have them wear a mask — not everyone else who is *not* infected.

"The CDC and the WHO's current recommendations are not based on *any* studies of this virus. And masking has never been used to contain any other virus pandemic or epidemic in history.

"There are, however, dangers to wearing a face mask, especially for long periods. Several studies *have* found significant problems with wearing masks. It can vary from headaches — caused by increased airway resistance — to carbon dioxide accumulation inside the mask — to hypoxia and severe life-threatening complications.

"I've mentioned that the only mask I wore doing operating was an N95 surgical mask. The N95 filters out 95% of particles, but it too impairs breathing and is associated with headaches. Trust me on this — I've experienced them. It is known that the N95, if worn for hours, can reduce blood oxygenation by as much as 20%. I've seen it lead to a loss of consciousness with nurses working with me. If someone is driving around alone in his car wearing an N95 — it could cause them to pass out and crash their car. In the cases of the elderly or anyone else with poor lung function — passing out and, hitting their heads can lead to death.

"Unfortunately, no one — not the CDC and not WHO — is telling the frail elderly and people with lung diseases — like COPD, emphysema, or pulmonary fibrosis — about the dangers of wearing facial masks — of any kind.

"And no one wants to say that the N95 masks can cause significant hypoxia — drop in oxygen levels — and substantial reductions in blood oxygen. People with cancer — especially if it has spread — are at a further risk of prolonged hypoxia because cancer grows best in a low oxygen microenvironment.

"And when a person is infected with a respiratory virus, they will expel some of the virus with each breath. If they are wearing a mask, especially an N95 — or any tightly fitting mask — they will be constantly rebreathing the virus, raising the concentration of the virus in their lungs and nasal passages. We know that people who have the worst reactions to the coronavirus have the highest virus concentrations early on. And this leads to the deadly cytokine storm — in which the immune system is producing too many inflammatory signals, which in turn, leads to organ failure and death.

"And lastly, no one should attack and insult those who have chosen not to wear a mask. Could be they're smarter than you."

"OK, let's move on," Porter said to the reporters.

"How did you catch COVID, Mr. President?" AP correspondent Doy Urbie asked.

"No one seems to know. As far as we can tell, no one else in the West Wing has COVID at this time. There have been three staff members in the residence side of the White House who *have* had it. However, I had no interaction with any of them.

"We do know," Porter continued, "that seven people I have been in contact with have had COVID — months ago — and have tested positive again — without symptoms — but why and how we're not sure."

"Out of an abundance of caution, Mr. President," Irish Leftwich of MSNBC asked, "don't you think you should mask up?"

"No, Ms. Leftwich, I don't. Mostly for the reasons I spelled out moments ago. This is a personal choice. Everyone knows I have had COVID and that I am now clear. So I will conduct myself accordingly. Make of that what you will."

National Public Radio's Miranda Bank asked, "The COVID Vax bill — which funds your FTL initiative to get a vaccine — has just passed Congress and become law — by overriding your veto. What is your reaction to that, Mr. President?"

"Disappointment. That bill — that law — besides funding the FTL program, also exempts pharmaceutical companies from any liability for the harm their product might cause. The way the bill is written this part of it isn't a separate part — so I can't use my 'Line Item' veto to strike it out. This puts Big Pharma in a class by itself — it can create a very beneficial vaccine — or a poison. Either way, they can't be sued by anyone their product may injure or kill. That's the part of the bill I didn't like. I hope no one lives to regret this law."

CHAPTER 36

"Mr. President," Defense Secretary, Victor Chesterfield said inside the PEOC with all the Joint Chiefs except Gen. Lee Evans, Chair of the Joint Chiefs, "you need to know that it was Military Intelligence — the National Security Agency that allowed you to win the Presidency in the election two years ago."

"Are you telling me I wasn't fairly elected?" Porter asked in shock.

"No, Sir. You were most assuredly fairly elected — but only because of Admiral Matthew Stott — Head of NSA and appointed by President Gibson."

"I don't understand," the President said.

"Your predecessor didn't know he was appointing a true patriot to head the NSA. He thought Admiral Stott was another of his Deep State players. Stott wasn't and never was. Admiral Stott intercepted and interrupted a sixteen-year plan to take the United States. The plan was Obama for eight years and Gibson for the last 8. However, at this point, before the next election, the military knew how corrupt the US Government had become, and so had the would-be government of the world. Other governments and other rulers — dictators and monarchies — all work for the New World Order corporation and have the best interest of the corporation at heart."

"So what exactly did — Military Intelligence — do?"

"They intercepted and corrected signals sent from automatic voter machines in key states. The machines had communicated with the New World Order and altered the actual vote totals. Vincent Sturges, the Speaker of the House, was supposed to win. It was the Republican's time."

"What do you mean, 'the Republican's time?'"

"Our two-party system is really a single-party system because of the corruption at the very top. Both of them are in on the New World Order. They are a part of and control the Deep State."

"That would explain why both parties were so pissed when I won."

"Yes, Sir. Their New World Order was supposed to come to fruition under Gibson. The bald Congressional Medal of Honor winner stayed seated as the president requested. You had set them back a few years when Gibson died, and you became president. And you've continued to disrupt their plans once you had the backing of the people. The Convention of States was the biggest wrench you threw into their well-oiled machine."

Porter's head was spinning. He shook his head slightly as he thought about what had happened since that night in Amarillo. He had taken the oath of office at the local airport almost five years ago and had become an unelected president.

"That's why Project Odin is so important." This was a statement and not a question from the President. "And GESARA and NESARA."

"Yes, Sir. We didn't tell you before because — all of this has been such a revelation — we wanted to — it's the wrong words but — 'spoon feed' you this little at a time."

"Little at a time has been almost more than I could swallow," Porter said.

"Sir," General Jovelen Door, Head of Space Force, said, "And that's why we've kept so much, the UFOs and all covered up. We were afraid of what letting it out all at once might do."

"I think the public is stronger than you might believe," Porter said.

"I've always thought so," said General Crane Felt, The Chief of the National Guard. But I have bowed to the wisdom of the others in this room."

"We all have," Gen. Denver Kimble, the Chief of Staff of the Air Force, said. "We could have been wrong, but we would rather err on the side of caution."

"And," the Commandant of the Marine Corps, General Knox Welch, said, "we didn't want to tip our hand to the corrupt media or the Deep State."

"I get that," Porter said. "What's our next move?"

"Because of the Pandemic, and the fact that you've had COVID, Mr. President," Victor Chesterfield said, "We think we need to rely on the Secretary of State to do some traveling. And by 'some,' I mean a lot."

"I warned him his job might come down to that. What does he need to do?"

"Get as many countries on board with GESARA as possible. And they need to understand that our NESARA does not overshadow the plans for the world."

"He is the man to handle that," Porter nodded. "Has he been fully briefed?"

"Yes, Sir," the Defense Secretary said. "In fact, his bags are packed. He only awaits word from you, Mr. President."

"Then I need to tell him 'go.'"

"I will admit to a small deception," Dr. Trench said to the media in the Press Briefing Room. "There was a real fear of lack of personal protective equipment for our front line health workers. That is no longer an issue. Regardless of how the President feels, and I have told him this myself, we feel face masking is important at the CDC. We believe we are following the science."

This was the broach-wearing Director of the National Institute of Allergies and Infectious Diseases answer to the question posed by Demona Enock if WOLF Cable News. The nation was split on their mask options as some governors and mayors had mandated masks and continued both isolation and social distancing.

"As we predicted, hospital overcrowding and massive deaths have become the norm," Dr. Trench continued. "All we can do is make educated suggestions. Piles of corpses are being seen in New York, Chicago, Houston, and LA again as we predicted. So, our stance on masks is to use them — outdoors, indoors in public places — and even in businesses — if they are still open. And continue to get tested.

"COVID is a pandemic. An extreme event — and it requires drastic measures if we are to get through it.

"But I do have good news," Dr. Trench paused for effect. "Because of President Randall's FTL initiative, we are only a few weeks, if not days, away from having a vaccine. And more than one. Two and maybe three different vaccines will be rolling out shortly. They must be approved by the FDA — on an experimental basis — but expect that quickly."

All the media seemed to have heard was what they reported, "Mask Up Indoors and Out," "Keep Getting Tested'," and "Vaccines Almost Ready."

CHAPTER 37

The portly and dark-skinned Secretary of State, Dexter Fetterman, phoned Porter about his overseas successes almost every day. In his mind's eye, Porter could picture the 55-year-old, 6-foot 3-inch man of deep thoughts and firm convictions as his slightly nasal-voiced came over the line. He was making progress — easier than he had expected. He was closing in on one-hundred countries as a part of NESARA, counting those Porter had talked to during the G-20 meeting.

When Porter hung up on the call, he opened his computer sitting in his Presidential Study. It was time for his weekly video call with his team of Medical Advisors.

"Good morning, Doctors," the President said.

"Good morning, Mr. President," was the reply for all online.

"As you see," Porter said, "I've added two members to our call. First is Surgeon General Vice Admiral Doctor Daton Westbrook."

The Office of the Surgeon General (OSG) is housed within the Office of the Assistant Secretary for Health. This person is the leading spokesperson on public health matters in the federal government. This is a presidentially appointed position and the operational head of the U.S. Public Health Service Commissioned Corps (PHSCC).

THE IMPEACHED PRESIDENT

Vice Admiral Daton Westbrook was in his black Navy Dress uniform. He wore rimless bifocals and, at 51-years-old, appeared to be in excellent health. His hair was black, and he had thick eyebrows over intense dark eyes. He had a square jaw and the look of a serious man.

"The other is my Presidental Physician, Brigadier General, Doctor Rosa Davanay.

The Physician to the President is the official title, but the office is known as the White House Doctor to the public. This physician is the director of the White House Medical Unit — responsible for the medical needs of the President of the United States, the Vice President, the White House staff, and visitors. The White House physician has an office inside the White House and oversees a team that includes five military physicians (one on duty at all times), five physician assistants, five nurses, three paramedics, three administrators, and an IT Manager.

One-star General, Rosa Davanay, 55, had a heart-shaped face, a flared nose, and a clef in her chin. She wore her olive-drab dress uniform.

"Everybody should have the resumes of everyone else here."

"We do" and "Yes, Sir," were the replies.

"All right. Where do we begin?" Porter asked. "The 'two weeks to stop the spread' has become nine months at this point. Has it helped?"

"I beg your pardon, Mr. President, but before we go there," Dr. Angelyn Cisneros from Florida State University's College of Medicine asked, "my first question, Is what happened to the flu? Down here, it appears to have taken a year off."

"I noticed the same thing," said Doctor Cyril Haines, professor in the Department of Pathology at Duke University in Durham, North Carolina. "I don't believe COVID has scared it away."

"According to the PCR tests," Dr. Ravi Khan with Dartmouth College's Geisel School of Medicine said, "which was never intended to detect viral disease, it shows more false positives COVID cases than negative ones. We have stopped using it."

"Then what test do you use?" Presidential Physician Brigadier General Rosa Davanay asked?

"Blood tests, and symptoms — fever or chills, cough, shortness of breath, fatigue, loss of taste or smell, muscle or body aches," Dr. Khan answered. "Have any of you examined the PCR test applicators?"

"No," answered all the others.

"We have. And have you realized they are all made overseas?" Tawny-skinned Dr. Khan was the chair of the Department of Microbiology and Immunology. "Look at them. There are microfibers embedded in them — material designed to be left behind in the nasal passages."

"I'll concede that most cases I've seen," said Doctor Haines from North Carolina, "present very much like the flu. But it is news to me about the fibers on the PCR tests."

"As I understand it," Dr. Cisneros said, "the PCR test is a molecular test that analyzes upper respiratory specimens, looking for genetic material — ribonucleic acid that causes COVID."

"Even Kary B. Mullis himself, the man who invented the test," said General Rosa Davanay, said, "in a video, I saw last night, claimed the PCR test should never be used as a tool in the diagnosis of infectious diseases."

"And common sense tells us that the more we test, the more cases we discover," Dr. Cisneros said. "And if the tests aren't accurate?"

"It all depends on to whom you listen," Surgeon General Vice Admiral Westbrook said. "Johns Hopkins University claims you can be vaccinated with a PCR Test — without knowing it."

"It sounds to me as if we shouldn't be using these tests at all," Porter said. "Am I understanding the consensus here?"

"Yes, Sir," came the replies. "And, Mr. President, I'll bet no one here has been able to isolate a real-live, purified sample of the SARS-CoV-2 virus — the virus that is supposed to cause COVID."

"No." "No, we haven't." "We've tried but haven't done it."

"So, what are you saying?" Porter asked.

"No proven virus — no disease," Presidential physician Brigadier General Rosa Davanay said.

"We've been chasing a phantom?" the President said in astonishment.

"I would say so," Dr. Khan said.

"Then all this isolation and lockdowns have achieved nothing?" the President asked again.

"If we look at what we've done by opening up here in Florida," Dr. Cisneros said, "and Texas — even North Dakota which never shut down — our reported cases are going down, and so are those in Texas and North Dakota."

"It seems to me these lockdowns have exaggerated cases in senior care facilities," Doctor Haines said. "And killed many small businesses."

"And the damage done to our young people," Dr. Khan said, "with this online learning and lack of social interaction — I believe we're going to see some serious developmental issues."

"And all for a disease that doesn't exist?" The President was stunned.

"Let's be honest here," Dr. Haines said. "It's harder to prove a negative than a positive. The country believes in COVID. The media stresses it every day — and charts the number of people who have died of it."

"Now we want to tell the public COVID isn't real?" the President couldn't believe what he was hearing or what he'd just said. "Then what are the vaccines for?"

"I think we have all been wondering that, Mr. President," Dr. Cisneros said, "but being the first ones to say it could cost us our livelyhood."

"I don't know if you understand how this works from a Public Health perspective," Surgeon General Vice Admiral Daton Westbrook said. "Dr. Trench has the power to do that. She provides all research funds, public — at universities — and private — by the pharmaceutical companies. Anyone who doesn't go along with her agenda will not only lose their funding — but will be damned in the press and on social media. In a word — they are done."

"What exactly is her budget?" the President asked. "I'm ashamed to say I've not looked at it."

"About one point six billion from Congress and another one point six billion from the military," the Surgeon General said. "And all the board members of her boards are also on her payroll."

"The public wants a cure," Porter said, "and they want it now. Can we tell them it's all been a hoax?"

"Their hope is in these vaccines, Mr. President," Dr. Cisneros said. "However, I'm not ready to put this experimental vaccine into myself. And I'm not going to recommend it."

"I agree," Dr. Khan said. "But I'm afraid we're in the minority."

"Let us examine these vaccines and see what's in them," Dr. Haines suggested.

"How many people are willing to wait and see?" the President said. "But I think you're right. That's the way to go." There was silence on the video call until Porter spoke once more. "If this turns out to be something bad — or even just a placebo, I will be the one who tells the public, 'We screwed up — big time.'"

CHAPTER 38

Today Baltimore, Maryland is an example of urban blight, decay, and crime. The historical and once-great city is now more infamous than famous. The Battle of Baltimore was a significant engagement during the War of 1812. The British bombardment of Fort McHenry resulted in a military failure for the invaders. However, during this fight, Francis Scott Key wrote a poem called "The Star-Spangled Banner." That alone should have endeared Baltimore to history.

While it is the most populous city in Maryland, as well as the 30th most populous city in the United States, it is thought of as an urban crime haven. The oldest US railroad, the Baltimore and Ohio Railroad — the B&O — was built there in 1830. It made Baltimore a major transportation hub. The city's port gave Midwest and Appalachia producers access to the Atlantic and the world. Baltimore's Inner Harbor was once the second leading port of entry for immigrants to the United States. In addition, Baltimore became a major manufacturing center. In the twenty-first century, Baltimore has become primarily a service-oriented economy. Johns Hopkins Hospital and Johns Hopkins University are the city's top two employers.

Miller Lefever was a corporal in the Baltimore Police Department.

Queenie Pool was the rookie riding with the twelve-year veteran, getting her first taste of being on patrol in Baltimore. They had stepped out of a sandwich shop in the mall on Ottis Street and were standing talking on the sidewalk. Northeast Baltimore was the city's most lethal neighborhood. A citywide average was one in three shootings being fatal.

A black Lexus with dark tinted windows approached the two uniformed officers from their left. The vehicle's windows rolled down, and at least eighteen shots were fired from the car at the two black officers, killing them both.

There was no "Black Lives Matter" protest that night, nor any succeeding night. The murder of the two officers only made national news because of its blatant daytime display of gang violence. The next day, the abandoned Lexus was located at the city's Thurgood Marshall International Airport.

"Defund The Police" banners appeared in the crowd during the funeral for the two fallen officers.

Two weeks after the Baltimore shooting, a freelance investigative reporter uncovered that Black Lives Matter had collected eighty million dollars since its inception. The first revealing revelation was that the organization's co-founder reportedly bought four luxury homes — each costing over one million dollars.

Further reporting by other sources claimed that BLM had transferred millions to a Canadian charity to purchase a mansion formerly owned by the Communist Party. The source of the funds was first claimed to have come from individual donors. Later, the narrative changed to imply that the organization's support came primarily from large corporate donations.

The organization's founders were committed Marxists. They named and backed radical left-wing members of Congress, especially Amelia Morris, the attractive 35, socialist, and bleeding heart liberal, from Mass. Known as the "new, bright shiny, thing," she was a media darling with outlandish ideas and poorly thought through pronouncements. Morris was also the failed VP candidate on the Democratic ticket against Porter.

Among other demands, the BLM called for the expulsion of Republican and Independent members of Congress for their treacherous actions. They even labeled all Republicans and Independents as white supremacists.

The organization demanded a full investigation into the ties between white supremacy and local police forces, law enforcement of every type, and the military.

They accused Israel of genocide and alleged that Israel was an apartheid state. BLM called on all the world's nations to boycott, divest, and sanction Israel.

In speeches, the movement's leaders wanted to lower academic standards for blacks from grade school through college. And they also demanded equity in all businesses.

This last demand was quickly withdrawn when it was pointed out that seventy-seven percent of NFL players were black, and eighty-one percent of NBA players were, too.

Traditional race haters, race hustlers, and prominent black political figures gave cover and support to BLM. However, they were careful to give equal billing to every organization they were members of. Outspoken black members of Congress who didn't toe the BLM line were all attacked as Uncle Toms. Conservative black radio TV and Internet talk-show hosts, even black academics, and Hollywood actors who didn't drink the BLM Kool-aid were the subjects to nasty BLM rhetoric and public shaming.

It was revealed that the predominant supporters of BLM ideals and protests were privileged white males. These were the people who were both figuratively and literally quick to kiss the feet of other black demonstrators and denounce their "whiteness."

Ideals of punctuality, cleanliness, ambition, and the nuclear family were denounced as evidence of white supremacy.

The movement began to experience unfavorable receptions as more and more became known about its focus and how it operated.

Not even former presidents and troves of celebrities' support could keep BLM from becoming exposed for its divisive slogans and actions.

"We never asked for donations," BLM leaders said on multiple occasions. "Corporation and individuals sent us donations — all out of *white guilt*."

But when they didn't file their income source and complete tax disclosure forms, they were dropped from several social media sites and banned from raising any more funds online. Four states threatened legal action. These were damaging — some expected death nel blows for the movement.

The public announcement for "experimentally approved" COVID vaccines was met with first excitement and then reservations. Two single-dose shots were available, and one two-dose version was rolled out quickly. They were made available to the nation's hospitals and then to individual physicians after a little over ninety days of development.

On his way to a Camp David weekend with the First Lady and selected staff, President Randall stopped to talk to the half masked and half bare-faced press corps. All were ignoring any semblance of social distancing. If any of the press noticed, none of them questioned the fact that the President was taking both the Surgeon General and the White House physician with him.

"Have you taken the jab?" MSNBC's Irish Leftwich called out.

"No," Porter said. "And to use your phrase, 'out of an abundance of caution,' I am in no hurry to take one."

"Why not? Your CDC recommends it, and your FDA has approved it," Buzz Yeager, middle-aged International News Key's White House correspondent, asked, his trademark tortoiseshell bifocals parked on his head.

"I've had COVID. I already have immunity. And it's true the CDC and the FDA work in my administration, but I am proud to say I do not tell them what to do. And if you'll read the bold print in their *recommendation* — note that I said 'recommendation' not rule, not mandate and not order, you'll find the word 'experimental' attached to it. Experimental means, 'Well, we *think* this might work.' But nobody knows what the effects of these vaccines are — especially the *long-term* effects. This is not Viagra — where the worst that can happen would be another deflated night — this could be like putting bleach in your arm and your blood system. I don't recommend that, nor does the CDC or the FDA. If you're willing to be a guinea pig and be first in line to take one of these — I consider you brave — naïve but brave. I want to study these things — and I have some people who are doing just that."

"And if they say it's Okay," asked the Associated Press's Doy Urbie. Urbie, forties and of middle eastern extraction, was respected by his colleagues and a thoughtful reporter.

"I'll see — if and when they say, 'Okay.'"

"But that could take months."

"I'm in no hurry to find out there are things in these vaccines I don't want in my body. I'm willing to give science the time it needs. I don't want to find these things out after I've already taken it. You know, sometimes the cure is worse than the disease."

With that, Porter joined the First Lady, and they crossed the South Lawn to the awaiting Osprey, Marine One.

CHAPTER 39

The Polish-born, seventy-nine-year-old American Cabal leader, Jerren Glowicki, sat in his Adirondack lodge near Panther Mountain in the New York state. The multi-billionaire conspirator against everything American was awaiting one of his minions.

Indirect lights dimly lit the room due to Glowicki's rare genetic skin condition, ichthyosis. It gave him red, scaly skin that was always painful and itchy.

Outside, a Lincoln sedan with dark tinted windows all around, pulled up to the lodge. The figure which emerged under the portico was Leon Nickleby, former Director of the F.B.I. The man had broad shoulders, white-blonde hair, and gray/green piercing eyes. President Randall had fired the always picture-perfect sixty-year-old. For the last two years, he lived in Brazil, where the US had no extradition treaty.

The butler opened the door, directed Nickleby to Jerren Glowicki's study.

"Are you up to speed on Irving Zaddach?" Glowicki asked with no preliminaries as soon as the butler had closed the door and left.

"I know he was arrested in New York, and they served him with both an arrest and a search warrant."

"He spent one night in New York, but now he's in Oklahoma City." Glowicki was leaning back in his chair, and except for breathing and talking, he didn't move. "They have three women who have given depositions against him and will testify at his trial."

"He will not live long enough to stand trial, will he?" Nickleby asked, taking a seat in front of the massive desk.

"That's for you to arrange. I have a clone on ice in a hotel in the city. What you'll need to arrange is to switch Zaddach with his clone and use one of our MK Ultras to kill the clone — in the cell."

"I can certainly do that," Nickleby said confidently. "How about his legal team?"

"He has a group of front-benchers — some of them ours and a couple who are simply good at what they do. They don't know we exist — and I don't want them to, either."

"Of course."

"They already have the proof that one woman who gave a deposition — her testimony would all be thrown out because the statute of limitation ran out last month."

"They are good."

"I want this to look like he's ready to go to trial — but was killed by a deranged inmate who didn't even know who Zaddach was."

Nickleby nodded his head slowly, considering the wisdom of the plan.

"Zaddach's been very valuable to us," Glowicki said, "and still may be in the future. We don't know what the FBI was able to get from what they confiscated in his New York mansion. Whatever it is, it won't hurt us but will expose some of the people whom we have blackmailed into doing our bidding."

"How about Seeley Caruso — the girlfriend?"

"She was more than that," Glowicki said. "She's on her way back to the island to clean things up there."

"Then I'll do my job — but what happens to the real Zaddach?"

"We'll get him out of the country and move him around for a while. He could end up knocking on your door in Brazil some sunny day."

"Are we concerned about any bombshell exposure?"

"Some. But none of it can be traced back to us."

"Anything else I need to know?"

Glowicki slowly sat forward for the first time and picked up a three-by-five card off his desk. He handed it to Nickleby.

"This is where you pick up the clone, and the MK Ultra asset is on the back."

The following Monday, Porter welcomed his Secretary of Health and Human Services, Talmage Goughenbaugh, into the Oval Office. The President shook hands with the fifty-eight-year-old Cabinet member and gestured him to a chair beside his desk.

"I'm going to fire Dr. Trench," Porter said, "and I didn't want you blindsided by it."

The squat Secretary Goughenbaugh stroked his goatee, but no surprise registered in his blue eyes.

"If you don't mind, Mr. President, I'd rather do it myself."

Porter was the one caught off guard. "I was trying to keep from giving you this dirty job, Talmage. Are you sure you want to do it?"

"It's my job, Mr. President. This is my Department — and she works for me."

"All right," Porter said reluctantly. "But do you know why?"

"She's been running the NIH and the CDC like her private kingdom for years. Judson Whitehead is her direct boss. But she had the Director of the National Institute of Health wrapped around whatever broach she happens to be wearing at the moment. She convinced him to give her sole authority to sign off on the budget items she controls. Over the years, she had accumulated more and more power of the purse — which translates into more power than any one person should have."

"I only recently became aware of that," Porter conceded.

"I'm sorry to say I figured it out a couple of months back — but I wasn't sure you'd back me if I confronted her — much less tried to fire her. She's become almost a J. Edgar Hoover in the CDC."

"Don't ever doubt that, Talmage. I asked you to be Secretary of HHS because I knew you to be an honest man."

"Thank you, Sir." Goughenbaugh stood, then had a question. "Do you want me — or someone else in my shop to take over the medical part of the daily Press Briefings?"

"Yes. I believe the Surgeon General is the right person for that job."

"I agree, one hundred present." The HHS Secretary paused before he opened the door. "Mr. President, you'll also have my resignation by the end of the day."

"I won't accept it," Porter said. "You haven't finished the job. We need a CDC and FDA we can trust. We deserve that as a nation. I want you to clean out the rest of your department, Talmage. Find out who should not be in the positions of power and who can be trusted. Then, if you still want to, I'll accept your resignation. But you have had years administrating public health. You, Talmage, are still the right man for the job."

CHAPTER 40

The news of Dr. Sinead Trench's firing was covered up by the murder of Irving Zaddach in his jail cell in Oklahoma City. Most coverage of anything related to the vaccines took a backseat to the killing. And even though Dr. Trench made herself available to any who wanted an on-camera or via Internet interview, none of the networks called.

The next day, when plainclothes FBI agents showed up at Dr. Trench's three-story Georgetown townhouse, they got no answer to their knocks and front doorbell ringing. One agent noticed the sound of a car running. By listening at the garage door, they realized it was a car inside the garage.

While one agent reported in, the other retrieved a battering ram from the trunk of the agent's car. Using it just as a DC Police car rolled up to the brick structure on Dent Place, NW. The FBI agents opened the door. However, the agents informed the patrol officer of what they suspected before entering. Then the agents announced themselves loudly as FBI and police. All three entered the residence with weapons drawn as the burglar alarm sounded.

When no one was located on the ground floor. The police officer who found the door to the garage called the two FBI agents. They discovered a relatively new dark blue Audi S6 sedan running in the single-car garage. One agent hit the automatic garage door opener while the other and the patrol cop went to the car with their hands over their noses.

A pair of garden hoses were heavily duct-taped to the dual exhaust ports in the rear fender. Both hoses were only uncoiled a couple of loops. The other ends of the hoses terminated with their brass fittings duct-taped to the back window, which were rolled down just enough to pass through the openings. The remaining parts of the window's opening were covered with double layers of tape.

Slumped in the front seat was Dr. Sinead Trench, PhD and MD, former Director of the National Institute of Allergies and Infectious Diseases. The fuel gauge was nearing empty, and Dr. Trench was dead. She was dressed in a yellow suit, the color of cowards, one of the FBI agents remarked, and a stunning emerald broach.

Her suicide did make the lead story that night in print and on TV.

"Mr. President, as you've read in the material we gave you, the Rothchild/Rockefellers have been behind every war for the past thousand years," the Secretary of Defense told the President in the Presidential Emergency Operations Center.

The only fresh face in the meeting was Admiral Matthew Stott — head of the National Security Agency (NSA). Stott was fifty-nine, average height and weight, an angular face, and deep-set, gunmetal gray eyes. The three-star Vice Admiral sat straight in his chair dressed in his black navy dress uniform.

"They fund both sides of every war?" Porter asked.

"They fund as many sides as there are. In our Civil War both the North and the South were backed by them — all the Axis powers and all the Allies in World War II. They are active in funding and developing weapon systems — behind the scenes of the military-industrial complexes throughout the world."

"War is good business," Porter said, grasping the point.

"Yes, Sir," Victor Chesterfield said. "And even more importantly, remember when we said they *are* the world's central banks? They are also the International Monetary Fund. This means they control all of the world's monies."

"They have the whole world in their hands?" Porter asked with a slight grin.

"It's more like they have the whole world by the short hairs, Sir."

"And this is where Project Odin comes in," the President stated.

"Yes, Sir." Victor Chesterfield pulled his empty pipe out of his pocket and stuck it in his mouth. It was a sign, Porter understood, that Victor was about to say something hard — but something that needed to be said.

"Mr. President," the Defense Secretary said, removing the pipe but holding it in his hand, "we know that you never planned to seek political office and only did so to force the Convention of States."

"I've never made a secret of that. In fact, I have been grooming Vice President Holyoak to run in the next election."

"Yes, Sir," Victor took a breath, "but your involvement in Project Odin means you are going to be needed beyond your current term. Things can't simply pause or stop while the Vice President gets to the point where she has what you've already earned internationally, Sir. And I'm not blowing smoke up your dress."

"I prefer to think of it as a kilt," Porter said to lighten the mood of the room, but no one even cracked a smile. The secure room was silent for a few moments before the President spoke once more. "Okay, I understand — and I'll tell the First Lady. She's going to be less happy about this than I am."

"We apologize for that," Victor said.

"But you realize elections are not sure things?" the President turned his gaze to Vice-Admiral Stott. "You'd understand that better than any of is, I presume, Admiral Stott."

"Yes, Sir," the officer said.

"And what if I don't legally win?"

"The polls have you at eighty-seven percent approval," Victor said.

"I don't believe in polls, and I don't trust them."

"You can have faith in these," Admiral Stott said. "We have verified their methodology and their accuracy."

"But before you even begin that process," Victor retook control, "Mr. President, there are some Executive Orders we want to suggest."

"I like those even less than running for office."

"Yes, Sir, we're aware," Victor said. He reached out towards Vice Admiral Stott. Stott handed the Defense Secretary two legal-size black leather folders. "Mr. President, these are some EOs we suggest you sign. The first," he gave the folder to Porter, "is entitled, "State of Emergency Regarding Federal Elections. It makes it a federal crime to, '...in any form, interfere, tamper, distort the process or intentionally miscount votes in federal election campaigns or elections by any nation, state, organization, company, group or individual, foreign or domestic.'"

Victor handed the folder to Porter.

"The second one is entitled. 'Continuity of Government.' It relies on the National Security Act of 1947, as amended. It says in part, 'It is the policy of the United States to maintain comprehensive and effective continuity programs that ensure national security and the preservation of government structure under the United States Constitution.

"'Executive departments and agencies, including the Executive Office of the President, must maintain the capability and capacity to continuously perform National Essential Functions (NEFs) — regardless of threat or condition, and understanding that adequate warning may not be available. Agency heads must fully integrate preparedness programs, including continuity and risk management, into day-to-day operations to ensure the preservation of the NEFs under all conditions.'"

"This second one, Sir, is to ensure that the government continues to function even if there is a fraudulent election or some catastrophic military attack."

Porter handed this folder to the President.

"We do not expect you to sign these at this moment, Mr. President. However, we would like for you to study them and obtain any advice you deem necessary. Only then we hope you will agree and sign these Executive Orders."

CHAPTER 41

President Randall and First Lady Deidra, were having breakfast in the upstairs residence of the White House when the telephone rang. Porter and Deidra exchanged looks. It was unusual for the phone to ring in the residence and even more odd that it would ring this early.

Porter wiped his mouth with his napkin, stood, and stepped over to the table where the ringing instrument sat.

"Yes," Porter said. He listened a few moments and added, "I'll be right down."

The President hung up and took a last sip of coffee as Deidra asked, "What's up?"

"I'm not sure," Porter told his wife, "but that was Vice-Admiral Westbrook, the Surgeon General. Evidently, my group of medical advisors has something they want me to know — right now."

"Then you'd better go." The First Lady stood and kissed the President.

"I love you," Porter said.

"I love you, too, darling," Deidra said.

THE IMPEACHED PRESIDENT

❦

When Porter came in, Graham Newcome was standing by the President's desk in his study. The encrypted video call was already up. The three medical advisors, Drs. Cisneros, Haines, and Khan were on screen in different windows. So were White House Physician Brigadier General, Rosa Davanay, and the Surgeon General Vice-Admiral Daton Westbrook. Porter took his seat and filled in the empty window on the screen.

"Good morning," Porter said. "What do I need to know?"

"Dr. Khan," the Surgeon General said, "You were the first one to call me. Why don't you begin?"

"Mr. President," the department chair of the Microbiology and Immunology Department at Dartmouth's School of Medicine said, "all of us have — unknown to each other — spent the night examining the vaccines. The one we were checking — which requires two doses to be effective — contains 99% graphene oxide."

"So does the single-dose vaccine my team, and I have been examining," Dr. Cyril Haines said from Duke University in North Carolina.

"GO, as it's chemically called, is in all of them," Dr. Angelyn Cisneros said from Florida State University's College of Medicine. "And this even though graphene oxide does not appear on either the FDA or CDC list of ingredients for any of the vaccines."

"Simply put," Dr. Rosa Davanay, the White House Physician, added, "GO is toxic to humans. It is a killer. Not always fast, but it is deadly."

"Then why is it in any of them, and why is it not listed by the CDC or the FDA?" Porter wanted to know.

"Perhaps," the Surgeon General said, "it's not listed because it is classified as a "trade-secret" — and because it is toxic."

"To be fair," Dr. Hines said, "graphene and graphene-related materials — what are called GRMs — have exhibited extraordinary physicochemical, electrical, optical, antiviral, antimicrobial, and other fascinating properties. But that doesn't counter its toxicity."

"I can see how that warrants the GRMs as potential candidates," Dr. Khan said, "for designing and developing high-performance components for the COVID pandemic. Graphene oxide can act directly on the respiratory system."

"When I Googled the MSDS + CAS number, it came up as being manufactured in China," Dr. Angelyn Cisneros said.

"Positively charged GO," Surgeon General Vice-Admiral Daton Westbrook said, "will destroy anything biological it comes in contact with."

"Now our other discovery," Doctor Haines said. The fifty-year-old MD and PhD closed his eyes for a moment and took a breath. When he was ready, he began. "There is also nanotech in these shots."

"What kind of nanotech?" Porter asked.

"Look at these slides." The professor from Duke, pressed a button, and his window was replaced with a gray magnified slide.

After peering at the image for a moment and enlarging it," the President asked, "A circuit board?"

"Yes, Sir," the voice of Dr. Angelyn Cisneros said. "Show your other slides, Dr. Haines."

The image shifted to a different shot. This one was again a circuit board in two pieces. The following slide revealed still another image of a circuit board. Dr. Haines ran through a total of nine slides, each with one or two sub-miniature electrical plates with lines and terminal points.

Dr. Khan said, "We have discovered these with every sample under magnification, down to almost the molecule level. And we also discovered that a frequency in the 5G range causes them to move. Two of the circuit boards in one sample moved and joined."

"My Lord," Porter said. "We have to stop this!"

Dr. Haines shrunk his window back to the size of all the other professionals on the call. "Yes, Mr. President. None of us know what these things do — but we know they ain't good."

"These vaccines should be pulled off the market," Surgeon General Vice Admiral Daton Westbrook said. "They clearly are not solving the problem."

Dr. Cisneros added, "We believe they are causing problems. Or will when activated."

"What we need to do is not just stop people from taking these shots," the President concluded, "but alert every physician in the country — ASAP."

"Yes, Sir," and "That's our advice," came the physician's reactions.

"Thank you — all — for your work and your willingness to bring this to my attention. I'll get this word out within the hour."

"Thank you, Mr. President," the doctors said almost in unison.

Porter clicked off the call. He picked up the phone on his desk. A moment later, when his personal secretary, Gwendolyn Jacobs, came on the line, he said, "Ms. Jacobs, will you please ask Ms. Fontana and Mr. Sterling to come to my study quickly?"

"Yes, Mr. President."

Porter hung up and turned to his Chief-of-Staff. "Graham, are you up to date on how to issue an Emergency Broadcast announcement?"

"I should get the manual, Mr. President."

Graham left in a hurry but slowed to a walk when he opened the outer door to the Oval office. The White House Communication team was there about to enter. He nodded to them in passing, and they closed the door once inside and crossed the Oval Office to the entrance of the Presidential Study. A third person was with them.

"Mr. President, we brought along Harris Ozman. Is that okay?" Director of White House Communications, Ms. Saundra Fontana, asked, sticking her head into the study.

"Absolutely," Porter said.

Ms. Fontana stepped in, looking severe and intelligent as always. She carried a reporter's notebook in one hand and wore a small gold cross on a chain around her neck. Behind her was Howard X. Sterling, the White House Press Secretary, wearing his usual starched buttoned-down shirt with dark tie and suspenders.

The photographer began snapping pictures with his Nikon D750.

Porter said with no other formalities, "We need to make an EBS announcement. Graham has gone to get the book on how exactly we do this. I am presuming you, Howard will voice this thing." He turned to Ms. Fontana, "Saundra, within the proper wording format, I need an announcement that says to doctors, nurses, and to the public — do NOT — repeat, do NOT — take any of the vaccine jabs. If you have, sit down and do not exert yourself. If you have any ill effects from a shot you've taken, do not panic, but report to the nearest emergency room. I want air time on all networks, over-the-air or cable — and using my podcast, too — to make a speech tonight at 8 PM Eastern. Period." Porter took a moment for Saundra to finish making her notes.

Harris Ozman continued to take pictures from every angle imaginable.

When Saundra looked up, Porter said, "I'll need Kenny Fallen to knock out a speech for me." Thirty-year-old Fallen had been the principal speechwriter for Vice President Sundee Ives. After almost two years as Porter's VP, Kenny came to work under Saundra as Porter's speechwriter when Ives left politics. He replaced Therese Herzog Porter's first speechwriter, who would now run for the governorship of Puerto Rico.

"I'll send him right in," Saundra said.

Graham came in with a small loose-leaf manual in an eight by four-inch ring binder. "I've got it," he said to Porter.

"Then let's get on this. And run it in a loop for a full thirty minutes, to begin with so everybody understands — then on every hour and half-hour for the rest of the day."

"Yes, Sir," they all said and left Porter alone with the photographer, who continued to work.

CHAPTER 42

"My fellow Americans," Porter said when the red light of the camera came on in the Oval Office, "do not — I repeat — do NOT take any of the experimental vaccines for COVID. They are toxic to the point of even death. Let me explain.

"The FDA approved three vaccines — but they were approved as "experimental" drugs. The CDC also approved them — experimentally. What that means is 'Take them at your own risk.' And remember, Congress saw fit to shield all the pharmaceutical companies from any lawsuits or damages by anyone who takes these shots.

"I learned this morning that all of these vaccines contain a substance known as graphene oxide. It's a chemical compound made in China — where our current COVID pandemic originated. When this compound is introduced into the human system, it is attacked by cells in our immune system that try to engulf it — even coagulate it. The result is that it generates clots and thrombi — fibrinous clots which form in a blood vessel or chamber of the heart. Also, it causes severe inflammation of the heart muscle.

"There are brain bleeds, bleeds from old scars, and bruising on legs.

"Women having their periods may fine their flow lasts for weeks.

Some post-menopausal women can begin experiencing vaginal bleeding. Pregnant women could experience miscarriages. Children close to someone who has been vaccinated might develop nose bleeds.

"Don't have MRI scans because these machines have powerful electromagnets which can affect graphene oxide.

"What do you do if you're already had one of these shots? Don't stress out! These effects don't impact everyone. And those who do have any of these adverse reactions may not have them severely.

"Regardless, go to an emergency room. The physicians there will know what to do. The medical information for doctors is available on the White House website. WhiteHouse dot com. There are some websites and other resources for everyone there as well. We have been getting this information out through every possible method to our front-line workers all day."

Porter paused and took a sip of water before he continued.

"The Surgeon General, the White House Physician, and I have spent all day researching graphene oxide. There are ways to treat it if you've taken a vaccine. I don't want to go into a detailed medical explanation here. However, this is serious and needs a physician's intervention. That is why we have been running the Emergency Broadcast alert all day.

"One fact we've learned is the 5-G cell phone network can cause complications. A person's body, thoughts, and emotions can be read and manipulated using 5-G technology.

"Several of the major pharmaceutical companies know this because they have worked on it with the military. Our military and the military of other nations.

"Some researchers believe that catching covid makes you dumber by seven IQ points. They also suspect that you will suffer adverse side effects that have not been fully explored if you have to be treated in intensive care and have been on a ventilator. If we had let the vaccination proceed, and you'd taken two or more doses, the danger would only be magnified. As it stands, there is research that predicts if you're pregnant, you have an 82% chance of miscarriage.

"And — " Porter started, but took a breath before he continued, "the other news is that each shot contains nanoparticles — nano circuit boards. Hundreds of them. We don't know what they do — but we do know that they are activated by frequencies in the 5G range.

"Fortunately, we've not made these vaccines mandatory for our military. We can only guess at the results if we had.

"The question is, who would want to inject as many people as possible with graphene oxide and nano circuit boards? People who want to control you. The answer is evil people with an agenda to depopulate, not just our country, but the world.

"Are there people that evil? Yes. They are the political and financial elites, the Illuminati, and secret societies of every variety. I honestly believe the goal was genocide on a global scale.

"Yes, there are such people. They are in our federal agencies, in Congress, and Hollywood. This isn't another Red Scare like in the 1950s. It's real — political — psychological, and physiological in design and in intent. This isn't anything you or anyone asked for.

"The CDC and the FDA are in my administration. I am the President, and I am a doctor. The buck stops here!"

He held the gaze of the nation as he stared into the camera for a moment.

"I want to ferret out those who don't have the best for our nation as their prime goal. You deserve that from your government.

"The simple fact is, neither our CDC, nor any other researcher, has been able to isolate or purify a single sample of the virus that causes COVID. How is it possible to create a vaccine for a disease we can't even prove exists? And how can it be done in such a short time? Yes, I called for an FTL effort — but what did we get? Something that was already in the pipeline? If so, *why* was it in the pipeline? Who knew this COVID was coming? And is it all about depopulation — genocide? I intend to find out.

"Thousands of doctors, nurses, and medical professionals of every kind, have been taken in by this entire COVID — what — hoax — conspiracy? Have you noticed we didn't have the flu this year? But the flu has the same symptoms as COVID. Our media has done everything possible to promote COVID. Twenty-four-seven, they have told us 'COVID IS COMING! COVID IS COMING! COVID IS HERE! COVID IS HERE!'

"The elderly were and are the most vulnerable. Underlying conditions, diabetes, obesity, heart disease, cancer — all these complicate any additional medical condition — like the flu. Thousands of people have died — in the hospital and at home — can their deaths be attributed solely to COVID. People who have been in an auto or motorcycle accident, been shot, or suffered any of a dozen other deadly events have all been reported as COVID deaths. Why? Because we were paying doctors and hospitals which treated COVID patients. We paid additionally for those who required ventilators. And we even paid for those who died of COVID.

"We packed elderly into already overcrowded facilities and then wondered why the illness and death rates skyrocketed in such places. We kept families away from their elderly, and this isolation created and compounded the effects of simply aging, making patients depressed and vulnerable to infections and diseases.

"And these graphene oxide vaccines quickly attacked the elderly's already compromised immune system. So did face masking.

"Face masks have had profound impacts on our children — both in their learning and in their social development. Children have the most robust immune system of us all. But some want to see them vaccinated, too.

"Say, 'No' — even 'Hell No!'

"Our health system has turned on us. We need to fight back — and so does the world. We need to take care of ourselves and those we love.

"Ivermectin, Hydroxychloroquine, and Remdesivir treatments have proven effective — against the flu — and COVID.

"Once again, I say to you, 'The buck stops here.' I take this responsibility with all the seriousness it deserves. But see to your own health and trust only those whom you believe you can trust.

"I hereby declare the COVID conspiracy over! No more mandates of any kind!

"And understand me — the only way you can get COVID is through the vaccine! It has to be injected into you! Do NOT take it!"

Porter took another long breath. When he was ready, he want on.

"You are free to choose to mask or not — to isolate or not — to exercise your full Constitutional rights. You are free and no one, not a governor, mayor, or city council can command you to do any of the things you have done to fight a phantom disease. I think washing your hands frequently and social distancing is good advice in flu and cold season. But you are free to choose even these.

"Research for yourself the use of vitamin D3, zink, and glutathione. Reports on all of them are on the White House website — WhiteHouse dot com."

"I will use the remainder of my time in office to see that our New FBI and the Department of Justice investigate and prosecute — as crimes against humanity — all those who knowingly foisted this COVID genocide — mass murder — plot on us. There are none so rich, so well connected, or in any way so powerful that they cannot avoid their guilt and responsibility. I include the media — professional medical organizations — even hospitals that knew this whole conspiracy was a lie."

Porter paused before he finished with, "Please pray for me — I am praying for you. And pray for the United States of America.

"Good night."

CHAPTER 43

As Porter told Deidra an hour later in bed, "This could be the end of my political career."

"And you just convinced me you need to run again," she tried to joke with him.

"After tonight, I doubt there will be much chance of that."

Seriously she said, "What else could you do? The pundits on TV and in the papers tomorrow they'll be saying, 'Of course, it's his fault. He sits in the big chair. It's his administration. It's time to put someone we can trust in the White House.' And so on and so on."

"You sound like you work for the drive-by media," Porter smiled in the dark. But the smile was also in his voice.

"I think you're going to be surprised."

"How?"

"The American people you think so highly of will see you accepting the blame as an act of bravery. Real politicians don't do that. The public will not hate you for it."

"Some will," he said. "I know I would if I'd already lost someone who took the vax. And those are the ones who'll they'll put on TV and quote in the papers."

"You know you did what was right, and you did it as quickly as possible," Deidra said as she snuggled up against Porter. "And don't give me your Abe Lincoln quote about angels sitting on your tombstone."

"That's exactly what I was going to say." he pulled her tighter to his side.

"I've already heard it," she said. "*Now, let go and let God.* He can handle it His way. And He will."

"I love you, Deidra," the President said.

"And you know I love you, too," she said, and they kissed.

※

※

※

True to Porter's predictions, he was crucified all night and on the morning talk shows. Each TV outlet found a grieving child, spouse, or relative who had nothing but words as bitter as their tears for the President by the morning. The morning anchors and early edition of newspapers were determined that Porter accept the blame for tainted and malicious vaccines as he had said was his.

On Capitol Hill, both the Democrats and the Republicans were rejoicing at what they considered Porter's catastrophic blunder.

One little read and never quoted paper, The DC Gazette/Tribune, carried the ice cream story. And even here, it was a minor item on page three. The headline read: "DC ICE CREAM PARLOR PEDO HQ?"

The story was about "I Scream For Ice Cream." It was a Northeast DC ice cream shop on the H Street corridor near the Rhode Island Avenue Metro. The supposedly family-friendly storefront business with "You name it" flavors was rumored to be a haven for pedophiles. A secret menu was supposedly in code. Orders placed by phone for later delivery could be translated into the pedo's type of child. For example, chocolate rum on a stick meant a naked black boy. Vanilla rum stood for a white boy. Cherry single dip in a waffle cone meant a white girl too young to have breasts. A double-dip would imply a developing female.

No one realized at the time that this story was about to blow the worldwide child trafficking scheme apart. It would implicate politicians high and low from both parties as well as powerful lobbyists and political activists alike. And it would all be a part of the next election cycle.

THE END

TWO FREE E-BOOKS

[Murder in Muleshoe]
If you were murdered would they try to find the killer or plan him a parade?

[Guns Along The Rio]
In 1858, two fresh-off-the-ranch 17-year-olds join the Texas Rangers. What could possibly go wrong?

GO TO: http://eepurl.com/dKEi_Y

ABOUT THE AUTHOR

Jack R. Stanley is an award-winning novelist, playwright, and screenwriter. As an officer and combat photographer in Vietnam, he earned the Bronze. He earned both his M.A. and his Ph.D. at the University of Michigan in Ann Arbor in Radio-TV-Film. His doctoral dissertation was on the TV series GUNSMOKE. Still married to his gifted high school sweetheart, Stanley was TV Area Head at The University of Texas at Austin's Department of Radio-TV-Film. He later moved to deep-south Texas and the Lower Rio Grande Valley for a challenging position with The University of Texas-Pan American. Here he taught Theatre-TV-Film for 30 years in the Department of Communication serving as Department Chair at U.T.P.A. for 11 years. He now lives in the Texas Panhandle where he writes his fiction. His webpage is www.jackrstanley.com.

ALSO BY THE AUTHOR

Novels

[Westerns]

Guns Along The Rio

West Of The Frio

A Hard Line Between The Rios

The Mormon Marshal

Along The Outlaw Trail

The Gavel and the Gun

13 Steps To Hell

Massacre At Going Snake

Incident At Lajitats

Pancho's Pilot

Return to Redemption

Occurrence At Latigo

The Hussy and the Hardcase

Some Men Need Killin'

Ode To An Outlaw

Crossfire At Daingerfield

[Science Fiction]

A New War

[Political Fiction]

The Reluctant President

The Reluctant Incumbent

The Reluctant Candidate

The Elected President

[Vietnam]

Through A Lens Darkly: Vietnam

[Mysteries]

Murder In Muleshoe

Corpse In Canyon

The Lovecraft Murders

Short Stories

Tales From The Alaskan Gold Rush

Klondike Justice

Dangerous Camp On The Kenai

The Winds of Skagway

Screenplays

6 and 10

The 7th Luger

Afternoon Delight

Angel's Revenge

Between Love And Murder

Blood Drive

Death Scene

The Defection of Grigori Dorsky

The Evil Eye

Fatty and Hearst

Gideon: The Horse That Saved Texas

Hell In Paradise

Hollowpoint

Holiday For An Assassin

Horse Thief Hollow

Incident A tLajitas

Love, Lust, & Life

Mom & Apple Pye
The Prometheus Peril
The Rape of Sarah Quinn
Reservations
River of Tears
Seven Reasons Why
The Thing About Love
The Texas Rattlesnake Murders
Too Good To Be True
The Vampire Rose
A Violent End
The Virgin Casanova

Plays

Antigone In Texas
Cyrano
The Last Virgin From Las Vegas
The Seven Keys
The Unwed Widow

Made in the USA
Middletown, DE
21 March 2022